STRANGE STORIES

Odd and Ends

ROGER MANNON

STRANGE STORIES

Acknowledgments

Here are a few things that made this little book of short stories possible.

First, of course, are friends (old and new) and family who read the stories, pointed out grammatical errors, and offered valuable suggestions to improve the work. Among these were:

Claire Fishback – a friend, former co-worker, and a remarkable young author. Claire's specialty is horror, but she also does fantasy and a little sci-fi. Check out her published stories and upcoming books at www.clairefishback.com.

Claire is unabashedly honest in her reviews of my work. She has repeatedly torn my stories apart and guided me in the reassembly. My stories are better because of her.

Donna Archer – Donna was my English teacher more years ago than I care to think about. She was only mildly successful in teaching me grammar and composition.

Her greatest gift was awakening in me the love of a good story. After all these years, she remains my friend and, still, my teacher. Donna helped edit Outsider and improved the final narrative.

Judy, my wonderful wife, and Laura, my daughter-in-law, and my good friend Heather Atton all contributed to improving these stories.

In second place are the various editing tools I use. Having an honest-to-God real live editor is best, but they cost money I don't have. So, hats off to things like AutoCrit, ProWritingAid, Grammarly, and RightWriter.

Then, of course, come the publishers of those magazines that are unafraid to solicit and publish stories from the many unknown authors of the world. Many also sponsor fiction contests and encourage those same unknowns to participate.

Glimmer Train, Tethered by Letters, Galaxy Press, Southwest Review, and others all read, judge, and, when appropriate, reward the works of new authors. Some offer free critiques of the submitter's stories. These critiques are invaluable to authors like me.

Preface

These are the stories found in the dark corners of my mind. Some are based on random thoughts that popped into my mind, seemingly from nowhere, or pondering the answers to impossible questions like "what happens to us when we die?" or, "Wouldn't it be wonderful if we could go back in time and skip the Great Recession?"

Others are birthed by reading books and articles to satisfy my curiosity about things like quantum physics, the birth and death of the universe, or the origin of the human species.

The Great Recession interested me a lot because it almost sucked the life out of me.

When I first wrote, most of these tales came to about a paragraph. But, the ideas stuck with me, lodged in the back of my mind, so I had to do my part and stick with the writing until they were done or as done as I could make them.

Strange questions and scattered thoughts do not make an entire story. So, like all authors, I fiddled with the ideas until I could fill in the blanks.

If you like these stories (or not), please leave a review – it's important.

Homecoming

The idea for *Homecoming*, the first and one of the shorter stories, crept into my mind after reading an article about veteran suicides.

The idea, a small, unformed concept, chased me into my dreams and back into my daytime musings again. They fermented over the days and weeks and, eventually, became a story.

This one is important to me. Just so you know, I spent the first third of my adult life in the U.S. Army. Two and a half of those years were spent in Vietnam.

I think about those years a lot. I think about Vietnam and my time there, the people I knew and surrounded myself with, and the people we fought.

I know the Veteran suicide rate is higher than that of the population in general. That knowledge, those thoughts, and my personal episodes of PTSD-driven night terrors led me to a story of how a troubled person could be led to leave this life. Might something better, familiar, welcoming be waiting on the other side?

1

Homecoming

Bobby Battles, nicknamed Battlin' Bobby by his buddies back in the bad old days when he wore Army green, wondered why vivid dreams of the war still chased him after all this time. The Army and the war, man-oh-man, those days were such a long time ago.

Now, 50-odd years later, he's just Bobby, and the only battles he fights these days are the ones in his nightmares.

He hoped (and sometimes prayed) they were nightmares but sometimes (often) wondered if the monsters he saw in those dreams might be real entities, something substantial enough to jump out and grab him by the throat.

His small handful of friends had just about convinced themselves he was more than a little crazy. Bobby heard them whispering when they thought he wasn't paying attention. He was beginning to believe they might be right. Sometimes he'd stare at himself in the mirror for long minutes and mutter to his reflection, "not right in the head, man. No, not right at all."

Bobby's baby sister, Samantha – Sam for short, loved him more than anyone could or ever would, or so she thought, but couldn't argue with those on-again, off-again friends. She knew crazy when she saw it, and she worried. She worried a lot,

Sam had watched Bobby go from slightly troubled to bat-shit crazy over the years. She knew the truth of it. Battlin' Boby Battles hadn't been OK since '75. The year he came home from his final tour of duty in Vietnam.

Bobby saw things, terrible things, mostly at night. Rebecca was sure they were nightmares, a lingering gift from Nam. She knew her brother didn't always think that was the case. He believed they might be something stranger than dark dreams, something real, something horrendous.

The once fearsome jungle fighter, Robert Wesley Battles, thought the things he saw were malformed creatures of the night, mysterious beings, phantom strangers coming for him.

Sometimes he saw the same dark, shadowy creatures or monsters or daydreams (whatever you want to call them) when wide awake right n the middle of the day.

No one but Bobby ever saw the strange things he did; no one else heard the loud, rumbling noises, like heat lightning off in the distance that frequently accompanied the visions. Bobby listened to those sounds far too often late at night, just before he drifted off to sleep.

Samantha knew it wasn't always easy for him to separate what was real from what wasn't. He struggled with the difference, and that's the truth. With time (lots of time) and practice, Bobby had just about learned to ferret out the real from the imaginary in his life. Most of the time but not all the time.

Sometimes, she'd hear him say precisely that right out loud after a beer or two. When he spoke those words, Sam would see fear flash across his face before he smiled and pretended he was joking.

Sam blamed it all on the Army.

Oh, she knew why he'd joined up. He'd told the story about a thousand times. He never lied to himself or anyone else and never once said he was excited to join the Army. No nineteen-year-old boy facing an ongoing war ever was.

For Bobby, enlisting was a simple choice, a thing he had to do. There wasn't enough money or food to go around. Enlisting didn't fix that, but it did make life less desperate for his mom.

Sam was just a baby back then, and their momma couldn't feed the four of them with a pound of bologna and half a package of Wonder Bread. She needed to pay the electric bill, and she needed cigarettes.

That's a sad fact about long-time smokers. None truly *wants* a cigarette or their mouth to taste like the back end of a trash can. Wanting took a hike a long time ago; needing took its place in line.

Bobby was the oldest, Sam was the baby, and Rodney was right smack in the middle. Rod was out of his epilepsy medicine, and all of us were worried about him. Where would they get all the food, the medication, and all the other stuff required by life if Bobby didn't find a job or get his shit together and sign up?

It wasn't as if there were a lot of jobs just waiting for him to show up, not in that dusty little Oklahoma town, population 280 and getting smaller every year. The tiny city was old and worn out. Businesses weren't hiring; they were closing their doors and never opening up again.

Comanche, Oklahoma, hadn't its face changed in several lifetimes and wasn't about to start now. Boardwalks dating back to the end of the previous century still stretched along Main Street.

Native Americans (Indians back then before us white folks figured out that was an insult) still stepped off the walkway into the street or the ditch to let whites pass by. Nothing new, not jobs, businesses, or people, were likely to show up any time soon.

Besides, Bobby had just graduated high school and knew he would get drafted soon. That was just how it was for young men (they were boys, really, just boys) back in the 60s, and he knew it.

He was born on September 25, 1952. It was 1970, and his selective service classification was 1-A, and he pulled a 9 for his lottery number.

Nine! Bobby was going into the Army or maybe the Marines if his luck ran out (they were drafting too by then) one way or the other, probably to Nam, might as well get it done.

One miserably hot and dusty Wednesday down near the end of June, he hitchhiked up to Tulsa, stopped at the closest Army recruiter's office, raised his hand, took the pledge, and boarded a bus for Fort Leonard Wood, Missouri.

He never said much about Basic Combat Training. Still, Sam remembered him telling her once, years later, after his tour of duty ended and he put away his dress greens and jungle fatigues," basic training doesn't really prepare a boy just figurin' out how to be a man for combat. To be fair, nothin' does."

He told her it didn't help any that the Army was doing what it always does; training their would-be soldiers for the last war.

Crawling through the mud and muck under barbed wire in a WWII battlefield simulation and getting screamed at by drill sergeants to "get your ass down" doesn't get the job done.

Neither does shooting at paper targets, picking cigarette butts and trash up off the ground during "police call." Nor does standing in a chow line while some hulk of a drill sergeant screams, "parade rest means clasp your hands together at the small of your back, not the big of your ass, soldier." Those words were often accompanied by the Drill Sergeant's baton poking you painfully in the small of your back while the Sergeant roared, "right there, soldier, Right. Fucking.There!"

Bobby never understood why the Army ever thought it would.

Less than a year after joining up, Bobby hit the ground in South Vietnam with just enough sense to remember to keep his head down, and his M16 pointed downrange. He mostly did both at the right time.

All these years later, he still remembered those days. "I'm not gonna pretend all 'em were bad ones," he said. "Some were, others were pretty good.

That sense of being part of something bigger than yourself, that ... what's the word, *camaraderie*, that's it, that's what old soldiers call it now, but, back then, I just knew it was a "we're all in this together" feeling."

That feeling hung in his mind, bringing back strong memories, a desire to find it again, and, he admitted, a feeling that he'd lost something good somewhere along the way.

Once, a couple of years after coming home, he told Samantha and Rodney, "Some of those lost days were just about perfect, or as close to perfect as I ever got.

We just lazed around in relative safety back at the base camp, hanging out at the enlisted men's club, drinkin' beer, and telling jokes." Those were the great days.

The bad ones had a lot to do with the stinking jungle, rockets, mortars, and Charlie tryin' to kill me before I killed him.

As Mr. Dickens might've said, those good days were 'the best of times.' Just doesn't seem like there was ever enough of 'em."

Bobby didn't talk so much about the bad days; he just said there were too fuckin' many of those.

When he did talk about those bad times, it was always the same story. Constantly crawling through rice paddies, walkin' through water up to their asses, or walking point on patrol, never knowing when some little dressed-in-black asshole was gonna pop up and take a shot at them.

He told of booby traps the crazy little shits put everywhere. Soldiers never knew when they might step on something that would blow their damn leg off, taking the nuts with it.

Those days never left him. So, here he was all these years later. Still livin' in a memory, or a nightmare fighting that long-ago war over again, day by day.

The truth is Bobby sometimes saw shadowy figures, like men (soldiers?), crawling through rice paddies or walking down a jungle path, slow-like, watching every step for something to jump out and kill them.

Those were memories, images from the long-ago past still stuck in his brain. He knew that. He might struggle with them, but still, he learned to shake them off when they came.

But, there's one thing he hadn't the slightest doubt about, someone or something alive moved around in the apartment above his.

It wasn't just imagination or bad memories come to life. He knew they were up there. He heard them late in the night when sleep wouldn't come and, sometimes, early in the day before the sun came up.

He believed someone was up there all right, moving around in the apartment above his. He heard the soft rumble of voices, the muffled sounds of movement as those above him shuffled about early in the mornings before the first rays of the sun broke the horizon.

Something about the noises, an ominous mixture of sounds, raised the hackles on the back of his neck.

The sounds ate into his brain and freaked him out; the shuffling footsteps, noises like fingernails scratching at the walls, a deep rumble like thunder over the distant mountains, and, too often, a soft, mournful moaning.

Those noises filled his apartment as he sat, listening in the dim light of early morning.

He told the landlord about 'em. She just looked at him, shook her head, and smiled a creepy little smile. It was the sort of look you might get if someone thought you had just walked out of a padded room and couldn't wait to get back inside.

The smiling lady told him the apartment was vacant; it had been empty for almost a year. He wondered if she didn't know or if she was hiding something. Finally, he thought maybe, just maybe, the noises he heard and his thinking the landlord was hiding something from him might be paranoia whispering in his ear, creeping back into his life.

Bobby was afraid to check it out, terrified it was just his brain tricking him again, more frightened that it might not be his damaged mind at all.

He was stuck. Too scared to look, more afraid not to.

The longer the noises persisted, the more he believed the unknown presences moving about in that apartment were here for him. He figured they were waiting for him to let go of his little chicken-shit-eyes-closed- hide-in-his-apartment dance and come to them.

Then last Sunday morning, he woke up early to a strange, disturbing silence. It seemed to him nothing moved on the Earth; even the air around him was silent, motionless. It was still dark out, an hour or two before dawn.

He had to go check it out, didn't he? So he did. He crept up to the door one floor above his and listened. Then he ran down the stairs taking two or three steps in each stride, and hid in his apartment.

Later that afternoon, after calming down, he called Sam and told her about his morning adventure.

"Sam," he said, "Thinking whatever mysterious people (creatures?) lived there might be gone, I walked up the stairs, quiet like, not making a sound, and tiptoed down the hall.

I leaned against the wooden door, my ear pushed hard against the grain, listening for anything to break the quiet.

I heard nothing except a deep silence and the thump-thump sound of my heart beating in my chest like a heavy-metal drummer playing for the devil, drumsticks flashing like lightning, fire sprouting from their wooden tips.

Long minutes passed. My ear ached from the constant pressure. My arms burned, and my leg muscles trembled from the tension of holding still for so long.

Still, I waited. I felt the sun move across the sky as time stretched; my heartbeats slowed, seeming to come once a minute, then once an hour.

It seemed an eternity passed; the universe died and was reborn before I overheard the soft thump of footsteps, the sound of a shoe (boot?) sliding across a thick carpet.

I heard many voices speaking together, but quiet-like as if from a great distance, and listened to a faint, repetitive whispering.

I couldn't understand the words if that's what they were. The voices were unintelligible, like the soft rustling of a million leaves as a gentle wind drifted through the trees.

Sweat beaded my forehead, and fear thumped in my chest. Stealing myself, pushing fear to the side, I knocked. Silence answered.

Suddenly, my courage vanished like smoke in the wind. I did not knock again. The fear in me swelled and filled my being. I was suddenly terrified that someone or some*thing* might answer. I fled, down the stairs, back to my dark apartment."

Sam listened and did not interrupt as the story spilled from Bobby's mouth. When he finished the story, she said not a word but picked up her iPhone and called Bobby's doctor.

Bobby didn't fight her on that. He just sat silently and waited while Sam made an appointment. Then he continued to explain.

"The sounds are intermittent, Sam; they come and go with the passing of the days, but my fear remains, never loosening its grip on me.

When I wake in the middle of the night, I talk to myself and tell myself it's just my imagination ignited by unreasonable fears, or worse, paranoia, the persistent effects of PTSD taking over my life.

I have never, not once, spotted anyone entering or leaving that apartment. Still, the noises permeate my place and fill my mind.

I sense an ominous presence living above me. Why would the unknown specter expose itself to me alone, through sounds only I can perceive? Why would it reveal itself at all if not for an evil purpose?

I wonder if it might be people, invisible people walking around, never seen but always heard or, perhaps, something else entirely, something alien to this world, coming for me."

Sam put Bobby to bed and sat beside him, holding his hand until he finally slept.

Sam was up early the next day, sipping coffee and pacing the floor. She kept checking her phone for missed calls. The anxiety followed her around the room until, finally, around mid-morning, Bobby's doctor called and told her she'd cleared a spot on her calendar for him.

Bobby resisted and said he was better this morning and needed no doctor. Sam nodded and said she understood but took him to the VA hospital anyway

Once there, she told Naomi Tallhorse, Bobby's long-time primary care physician, that he'd started hearing things again and asked if she should increase the PTSD meds. Dr. Tall Horse smiled and said, "why don't we let Bobby tell me what's going on." Sam blushed, "oh, of course," she said.

Samantha liked the doctor a lot. She seemed like a fine, compassionate lady and a great doctor. Naomi Tall Horse filled many shoes, full-blood Cheyenne, a full-time VA doctor, and a part-time tribal medicine woman.

More importantly, she listened to Bobby, seemed to understand, and never pushed the meds. She suggested that his visions might be related to PTSD and told Bobby the medication might provide some modest relief.

"Relief," Bobby thought, "I could use a big helping of that!"

Booby was hesitant to tell the story, so Samantha told the doctor about the unusual noises Bobby heard, although the apartment they came from appeared to be empty.

Bobby picked up the story from there. He told the doctor how much the sounds frightened him and made him wonder if someone or something was stalking him.

After he said those things, he smiled a little smile, looked at the doc, and said, "I know how weird that sounds. I ask myself if I'm just over-the-top paranoid, and there's nothing to this whole business."

While Bobby talked, Doctor Tallhorse stared at him, unblinking, her obsidian eyes probing like she was looking straight into his brain, reading his thoughts, scanning his memories.

She nodded once and told Sam she needed to speak to Bobby, alone, for a few minutes. Sam didn't like it, but she left the doc's office, mumbling under her breath as she walked away.

Naomi Tall Horse reached out, held both Bobby's hands, studied his face, touched his mind with hers, then spoke.

"White man's medicine will tell you that you suffer from PTSD, and they would be correct. But, there is something else here. It's rare, but fear can become real, and manifest itself as a creature as real as you or I. That might be what you sense."

"Come on, Doc!" Bobby said, "How can I make something real out of nothing at all? Doesn't seem possible to me."

"Believe what you will, Robert. I know the world is stranger, more . . . complicated, I suppose, than most people understand. I am not telling you the things you see and hear are merely your fears come to life. I AM saying it is possible.

There may be another answer. My people, the Cheyenne, and many other tribes believe humans, especially people in great mental or physical distress, can send their energy out into our mysterious universe seeking help and relief from the darkness that lives in our souls.

It is also possible that your visitors are something else, something you have called, and the calling has been answered.

"I cannot name what has to come to answer your call, but I can tell you your fears may be misplaced. The presence you feel may be the answer your spirit demands and so desperately needs to soothe and heal the damage left to your mind and body from the war you left behind so many years ago.

Let that be your hope."

Then the doc released Bobby, let go of his hands. He felt her mind leave his. For a moment, he wondered if he was dreaming again, making shit up out of nothing at all? How the hell could he have felt her inside his mind?

He shook his head and thanked her for her words because, for some strange reason he couldn't point to or put a name on, he felt more at peace, calmer, and stronger than before their meeting.

The doctor increased Bobby's daily prescription and told him it might help ease his anxiety. She said he should call if he ever needed to talk.

Bobby wouldn't. He sometimes wanted to, but he never did. Anytime he picked up his phone, the words just dried up and turned to dust in his throat.

Bobby was still a little angry that Sam would suggest he was losing control. Sure, he'd often heard noises echoing through his mind once, years and years ago, not long after coming home from Nam.

The sound of bombs shattering the night, rockets, mortars, and automatic rifles rattling through the jungle chased him into sleep and followed him into horrible nightmares. So many times, he woke, trembling and screaming, sweat flowing out of his pores like rivers of fear.

He would sit alone in the dark heart of the night as the visions and sounds of war slowly faded from his mind. Too often, he could not go back to sleep, afraid the nightmares would find him again.

Back then, no voice muttered his name, and nothing called out to him. There were no whispers in the night, no footsteps walking his way. The sounds that jumped out of his memory and took his breath away, scaring the hell out of him, were the hammering of rifle fire, the shriek of rockets, the screams of the dying, and the suffocating silence of the dead.

Bobby loved Sam. Loved her as much, or more, than anything in his long life. She was his beacon against the night. Still, he wasn't happy about her "hearing things" comment to doctor Tall Horse. Even though he had to admit he heard something, listened to strange sounds in the night. The noises no one else seemed to hear.

He recalled a time, years ago, after the gunfire faded from his mind, he had heard unusual noises, sometimes imagined strange, terrifying images, things from his nightmares invading the daylight hours. The sounds echoed through his mind, a rumbling noise deep inside him, shaking his mind while the outside world remained quiet.

That whole "hearing things" period hadn't lasted long. It was like the last vestige of the war leaving his mind. He'd always understood those sounds weren't real. He found it easy to separate them from everyday life. Bobby knew they were only remnants of terrors seen and felt far away in a lost past.

The bad dreams were always the worst of the terrors, far worse than the brief life of those fading memories. Back then, the sounds, echoes of war he called them, were nothing compared to the night terrors. Those times when something dark and ugly, a formless, nameless monster, barely glimpsed but coming ever closer, chased him out of bed and left him cringing in the corner.

Whatever was going on now was different. The unusual noises always came late in the evenings, in that strange, twilight place that lives between full consciousness and the edge of sleep.

It didn't seem like voices. Bobby knew if it was a human (or inhuman) voice, it was the synchronous sounds of many. It was the voice of thousands screaming into the night. The noise, a pulsing, rumbling roar like ocean waves crashing against the beach in a storm, entered his mind and scrambled his thoughts.

The trouble was, Bobby believed the sound *might* be a voice, or voices, the combined utterance of many speaking as one, talking to him, telling a story he would understand if he just listened harder.

Bobby kept his mouth shut, didn't tell Doctor Tall Horse or Sam, but he was already taking a double dose of the PTSD meds each day. It helped a little, but not enough. Nothing helped enough.

Some days he thought maybe he should double up again.

He believed Sam had it all wrong. Yes, he still had infrequent nightmares. He still dreamed of wading through rice paddies and pushing through thick, steaming jungle bush, forcing his way through clouds of flying, biting insects and the always-present stink of the place, forever running for his life or fighting the invisible Cong.

At times, the rhythmic clattering of AK-47s as enemy rounds poured into the base camp shook his mind. He sometimes relived the screaming of incoming rockets and the roar of exploding mortars as they tore apart canvas tents and shredded the few brick-and-mortar buildings.

Sometimes he would even wake from the nightmares with the coppery scent of blood thick in his nostrils, the taste clinging to the back of his throat.

Bobby had had those dreams for so long that they'd become old friends. He expected them, hated them, lived with them. Lately, he wondered if, maybe, the pills worked at all.

The sounds he heard recently, those noises from above, those new sounds were different, something new. They scared him more than he admitted, even to himself.

There was a moment, only a few days ago, he was pretty sure he might've seen whatever lived up there in that empty apartment above his. He didn't tell Sam. What he saw was too strange; telling would've frightened her, caused her to worry more than usual. He figured she needn't be concerned about his sanity. He worried enough about that himself.

What he saw scared the shit out of him. He was afraid he might be losing his mind but was more worried that he wasn't. He feared the curious shapes he glimpsed floating through the hallways were not hallucinations but something real.

Bobby had watched as strange, distorted shadows, dark as a moonless night, drifted through the building, paced the hallways, and crept up the stairs.

The shadows appeared where there was no light to cast them, no people to make them. They flickered at the edge of vision, like stars in the night sky seen through gaps in the clouds, there and then gone.

Glimpsing those strange shadow-like shapes cemented belief in his mind. He was sure something was there, some mysterious entity or unknown force. Still, he didn't understand what those dark, creeping shapes might be or what they wanted. All he knew was they scared the hell out of him, and over the last few days, the fear woke him, trembling in the night.

He knew something unknown and frightening lived above him. His belief was a transient certainty. One moment he wondered if it was his imagination gone wild; the next, he was sure his nightmares had come to life.

He spent minutes and hours wondering if the dark, ghostly beings he watched were real. Mostly, he was afraid, deathly afraid the shadow-shapes were real and were there for him.

Sam called just as the sunlight started to die. She said she wanted Bobby to come live with her, but he couldn't do it. She was his only family, and he understood her desperate need to protect him and keep him safe, even from himself.

Bobby just could not do that, even for Sam. He couldn't be around too many people. People were hard. He still needed to know where people were, who might be behind him, and how to get away if it came to that. He couldn't do that with others around him. He told himself, "one other is one too many. I am better, safer alone."

Sam insisted. Bobby lied; told her he would think about it.

Late one afternoon, the landlord showed the place upstairs to a young couple. Bobby knew she was going to show it and waited until she opened the apartment door, and led them in.

He casually strolled by and peeked inside. The place was empty. He saw nothing, no furniture, only bare floors, barren cupboards and countertops, windows without curtains.

The apartment was empty except for the evening shadows slowly creeping across the walls. Bobby thought, "how can that be? I hear them. I know I do."

He returned to his apartment, lay on the ragged old couch, and thought about the sounds that woke him in the night. Once again, his mind turned to the images of the dark, distorted silhouettes he had seen as they slithered through the hallway.

He wondered, "could Sam be right? Is it my PTSD, alive and grown worse, coloring my perception of the world and everything in it?"

Samantha called while he was watching Chicago Fire. They talked. "Did you take your medication," she asked.

"I did, Sam. I always do."

"I worry about you, Bobby. I can't help it."

"I'm fine, sis. I just let my imagination get the best of me. I'll be more careful, tell you the moment anything changes, you know, if I get a little paranoid again. I promise."

"Call me if you need me. I'll come right away."

"I know you will. I promise I'll call if I need you."

"G'night, Bobby."

"Night, sis."

He flicked through the channels looking for something to watch; nothing caught his eye. It was getting close to his usual time for the pills, the ones that were supposed to protect him from the nightmares but didn't.

Hoping tonight would be a good night, Bobby counted out four of the little capsules, put one back, and washed down the other three with ice-cold water from the fridge.

It was still too early for bed. So, he picked up a book, stretched out on the couch, and continued reading about a horrible flu-like illness that killed off damned near everyone on the planet, leaving only small pockets of good and evil folks to fight for the future of the world.

Bobby must've fallen asleep. The sound of someone, *something*, walking around upstairs woke him. He looked up, his mind still halfway inside a forgotten dream, and noticed a long, black shadow gradually seeping through the ceiling, coming into the room from above.

It slid down the wall like a slowly spreading ink stain. The shadow creature fell into his apartment and lay crouched on the floor between the couch and Bobby's LazyBoy.

The shapeless blob began to flow and change like lava. It bubbled and bulged, slowly forming itself into a distorted human silhouette.

Arms fell from narrow shoulders, almost touching the floor. Pencil-thin legs, long pointed fingers, and a deformed, bulbous head formed, solidifying from the molten flow, like shadows on the wall filling out and coming to life.

And, like the dying embers of a campfire, a hazy, reddish light flickered in its pinprick eyes and broad mouth; the glow cast dim shadows in the darkened room.

The too-wide mouth opened, and the red glow changed, grew bright, the color now a sizzling blue like the light of a blowtorch. Then, like the beacon of a lighthouse, blinding rays poured from the giant mouth and flickered briefly before fading away.

A deep, hoarse voice spoke, whispered Bobby's name, and, the words falling slowly from its mouth, like honey dripping from a spoon, said, "folllloooowww meeee,"

The dark creature raised one long, black arm, and pointed its needle-thin shadow finger toward the door.

The mysterious entity drifted to the front door, paused, then, stepping forward, the dark silhouette passed through the solid wood of the doorway as effortlessly as sunlight through a windowpane. Trembling, Bobby opened the door and followed.

The shadow man-thing, moving slowly, floated down the hallway like coastal fog drifting in a faint ocean breeze.

It crept up the stairs. Bobby walked behind, strangely calm, controlling his fear. The door of the mysterious apartment stood open; the creature slipped inside.

In a dream-like trance, Bobby hesitated. Seconds later, afraid of what was happening but knowing he needed to understand, he stepped over the threshold. The room was as barren as before but for the shadows on the wall.

The shadows, crystal-clear angular outlines of a faintly human form, seemed to greet him, each nodding and bowing. Like static from a poorly tuned radio, hissing voices filled the empty room. The hissing shifted, the static faded, and the noise merged into a single mighty voice speaking clearly. The message pierced Bobby's soul as the words washed over him. "Welcome Home!"

The far wall vanished, replaced by a bright swirling light, cyclonic, like water circling a drain. The shadows flew free, one at a time, entering the storm.

Lightning flashed blue-white, its forked arms reaching out, touching each shadow-man as they passed through the radiant barrier to whatever destination lay beyond the light.

With each flash of strobing light, the black countenance of each shadow diminished, revealing glimpses of haggard faces, some familiar, some not.

Every face was different, but all the same, streaked with dirt and muck.

The dried sludge clung to their brows and cheeks, mixed with the greens and browns of camouflage paint. The same weary determination marked each face.

Briefly, Bobby saw faint images of combat boots, worn and torn, rotted in spots by jungle heat and humidity, tiger-striped jungle fatigues grown thin and shabby with jagged tears, Boonie hats soggy with sweat. Spattered blood clung to the uniforms and faces in various places.

At last, he understood. Thinking of Sam, setting her free to live her life, no longer needing to worry about him, fear fell away.

Bobby, at last, understood. He was set free. He knew he could leave memories of the long-ago war, the smell of rotting jungle vegetation, and visions of the dead and dying behind.

That life passed away long ago. It was time for him to let it go. Lightning flashed and called his name. Then, with a last look back over his shoulder, Bobby smiled before he, too, stepped into the light.

It was time to go home.

END

A Ghost Story

The following story is the fault of *The Walking Dead*.

Watching the show, I wondered, "How do you know if you're dead?" "Do the dead even have a working brain, thoughts?"

Those weird questions led me down a twisted path to the truly dead. You know the ones I'm talking about, they are the lonely dead lying in a remote graveyard somewhere, the remains of their physical bodies feeding the worms.

I thought about their ghosts - if such a thing as a ghost exists. I asked myself what life might be like to live as a wandering spirit flitting around the world.

Late that night, my mind, set loose to drift in that weird realm that exists between sleep and not-sleep, conjured a crazy(ish) answer to those questions.

Here is *A Ghost Story*.

2

A Ghost Story

How do you know when you're dead? The obvious answer is, you don't know shit when you're dead because, well, you're dead.

Someone more religious than, say, me, might answer, "you'll know because you'll wake to find yourself standing at the feet of God."

I've got my doubts about that but admit there's a possibility (slim as it might be) you could meet Jesus or any of about a dozen others.

Which God you might encounter in the afterlife depends on which mystical personage your specific religion chose as the Master.

An atheist might echo the most obvious answer, adding that you, the physical person you once were, had now returned to the dark oblivion of non-life.

Maybe I'm a slow learner 'cause it took me a while to figure it out.

I don't think much about my death anymore. I mean, I hardly remember the whole thing. Oh, I have this vague sense that I was confused, then terrified (only for a second or so, because the entire affair was over pretty fast.)

When I attempt to recall the event, I have this sense of chaos, people screaming, running for cover every which way, some falling to the ground, some hiding behind the trees and hedges.

I was in a world of frantic turmoil and then, searing heat eating at my body, followed by a solitary flash of extreme pain lasting both a single moment and a lifetime.

My ghostly brain resonated with the sound of bullets screaming through the air. It conjured the blistering heat of explosions and fire and generated imagines of blood falling like rain from the sky in a cloudburst of carnage.

Faint echoes of near-forgotten memory wash through my psyche. Among them, the rising crescendo of screams pummeling my mind, the pounding footsteps of running feet.

Before darkness swept me up and took me away, the riotous sounds of tragedy swept over me, pounding my body. Then there was nothingness for a long time.

Maybe for a long time, I'm not really sure about that. What is the passage of time to the dead, after all? I just know I was gone until I wasn't.

The precise moment of my demise and the circumstances surrounding it never coalesce into a sharp memory or become clear and real, urgent in my mind.

The doorway to death and the fleeting moments both before and after remain locked away.

Whatever happened is separated into the chaos before and the darkness after. The complete memory of what happened and the precise instant of my death is impossible to retrieve. Perhaps that is as it should be.

Time passed. How much, I don't know. At last, scattered memories began to come together, merge into my consciousness.

Sorting through the fractured memories, for a moment, I wondered if I had been military, maybe in Afghanistan or Iraq, fighting for my life. Yet, that idea didn't fit with the fragmented memories beginning to form in my mind.

The new recollections developed around the idea of a busy college campus. Too-short visions of long, never-ending days and nights spent in libraries and laboratories sorting through impossible ideas emerged.

The least fragmented memories available to me were about the mysterious quantum world, the ideas and mathematics behind the possibility of parallel universes, and quantum vibrations' potential relationship to consciousness.

I retained a dim concept of the many-worlds theory and remained entranced by that strange circumstance called quantum entanglement.

Vivid images of me, disheveled, needing a shower, hair like the twisted remnants of dead cornstalks, scribbling on a whiteboard covered with exotic equations bubbled into my consciousness, filled my phantom brain.

With some confidence, I now believe I was a teacher or professor of quantum physics or, perhaps, a graduate student studying the quantum realm, the nature of time and space, of reality itself.

The truth is, I was surprised and more than a little confused by my reappearance in the world. If appearance is the correct word. I see everyone. No one sees me.

I didn't realize I was a ghost at first, wasn't entirely sure what was happening. I woke or came into being wearing my favorite pair of jeans and Eric Clapton t-shirt, the one from the Journeyman Tour, Eric's stern face painted large, staring out at the world.

At first, I thought the idea I might have died in some horrendous tragedy could have been a terrible nightmare; perhaps a fever-dream brought on while thrashing and sweating through the agony of an awful illness.

I imagined I was in the early stages of a slow recovery, my mind clearing as the illness receded and the fever abated.

I could feel my body surrounding me. Soon, my mind would clear, and life would return to normal. I tried to believe that.

Except for the half-formed terrifying memories (which might well be the remnants of a nightmare driven by a hellish temperature) floating around inside my head, I felt unexceptional, ordinary in every way.

Ordinary may be an exaggeration.

I realized for some undetermined length of time; I had been here in the world, but not.

While in that missing piece of time, I was lost, with only a dim awareness of self, inside some endless place (my mind?). That condition cannot, in any circumstance, be called an ordinary event.

After waking, coming into myself, and feeling not the tiniest indication of illness in my body or mind, I wandered the streets of downtown Denver on the lookout for old friends.

I smiled and spoke to people on the 16th Street Mall as I walked along the avenue. No one looked my way or answered my greeting.

The idea that something very odd was going on crept up on me. It took me a few minutes before I, at last, realized the folks strolling the streets couldn't see or hear me. They were oblivious to my presence.

It was as if some mystical force, a gentle wind made of an indefinable power, like an electromagnetic field, moved them around me.

Like the browned and brittle leaves of winter blown about by the cold wind, tumbling across an empty graveyard, constantly circling, forever close to but never touching the tombstones, people approached, stepped close to me before the mysterious force pushed them away.

One by one or in small groups, strangers came close, stutter-stepped a bit as if pushed aside by some invisible barrier, then spun away.

I'd walk straight towards the groups of people, knowing they would have to acknowledge my existence or run me over. I was hungry for someone, anyone, to recognize my presence, to smile at me or say hello.

But, before I could raise my hand in greeting, they would turn aside, their movements sudden, awkward like a puppet jerked away its strings. The strangers on the street didn't seem to notice their clumsiness.

Spinning aside, avoiding contact, they would take a moment to peer into a store window or take a small, subtle step to the side like they were skirting a dog turd on the sidewalk.

The force that caused them to avoid me appeared to work on a subconscious level, an automatic response to a presence not felt but intuited.

After several attempts to be seen, acknowledged in some way failed, I turned towards a coffee shop window and observed the reflection of the passing crowd. I could not find myself among the comings and goings of the walkers.

That's when I first realized the dim memories of explosions, fire, and terrified screams were real, the hallmark of dark violence falling upon my small piece of the world. The still-shadowy event had changed me in some peculiar fashion.

I felt disconnected from the world I knew, ripped from the fabric of that universe by an inexplicable power, and thrown into a nearby parallel existence, one of the many possible realities I had studied for so long. Had something more terrible than that occurred?

Was I no longer among the living? If so, might death just be a single step from this life to another, through an invisible doorway into a different universe?

Perhaps I still lived as a shadow of my former self, an invisible presence in the world I once inhabited.

Or, maybe, now I existed in a nearby place, a mysterious location, similar to but not quite the same as the universe I once occupied. A realm close to (side-by-side, in fact) but not part of the world I previously knew.

It was a world I could observe, like a man standing on the dark side of a one-way mirror, I could watch the people, animals, and structures of this place, but they remained unaware of me. I could not interact with them, nor could they with me.

Whether this place was my old world or some new nearby reality remained unknown, but the creatures living here could not see me. I was a ghost to them.

I accepted the possibility that I might not be alive at all, although my consciousness continued to exist in some strange fashion.

Perhaps I'm not an observer from an alternate plane but, indeed, a ghost, an unseen remnant of my former physical self.

Whatever the case, my psyche continued to exist, my thoughts real, as real as the body that once held my spirit. My mind still observed, explored, asked questions.

Late that first evening, unanswered questions roiled my mind, and possibilities bubbled in my thoughts like lava gurgling up from an active volcanic cauldron.

Struggling to understand this new existence, I strolled down 10th Avenue towards Osage Street and one of my old hangouts, the Buckhorn Exchange. I guess I was just looking for assurance in a familiar place.

For a moment, I thought, no, I hoped, all the day's strangeness might be a sign of mental distress or a fugue, a psychological disorder from which I might abruptly recover. Wishful thinking, I know.

I stood outside the door, decided to experiment, reached out to touch the door handle, and tugged. The door moved towards me, only a fraction of an inch, but proof I must have some physical presence.

In a burst of inspiration, I let go of the handle and stepped up close to the door, leaned forward, pushed through it. It was like passing through a faint ocean mist, one cast about on a breezy shore.

Some small resistance touched at my face, cold, like the icy fingers of a brief October wind tugging at my hair, then I was through, standing inside.

I accepted this as proof that living or dead, here in this familiar world or existing in some other strange reality, I was a ghost-like presence to both the structures and peoples of this place.

I also accepted that all things being equal, death was the more likely scenario, more probable than an unexplained excursion into a parallel universe, a place hinted at but never proven by my beautiful equations.

On some level, of course, I must've known none of what I had experienced might be real. I could be insane, just another crazy person trapped inside a psychotic episode. How would I have known the difference?

I didn't feel crazy, refused to accept the idea I could be, and, instead, became yet more convinced that my physical body was gone forever.

I believed I continued to live only as a phantom, dead, but still attached to the living world for some unknown purpose.

Inside the Buckhorn, my senses woke to the scent of T-bone steaks sizzling on the grill, onion rings frying in boiling oil, perfumed women, and aftershave on men, all mixed amidst the noisy chatter of friends sharing their lives.

I wandered towards the grill, stood over the seared meat, watched the thin layer of fat around the edge bubble and pop; small smatterings danced like tiny raindrops across the hot metal plates.

As the juices flowed towards the grill's grease traps, I leaned forward and inhaled the delightful fumes. The aroma-filled vapor of the cooking meats entered my nose, battered my senses with incredible memories of a life once lived.

I tasted the flavor in the back of my throat and experienced a sense of fulfillment as if I had completed an intricate and pleasing meal.

Standing there, invisible to all, enjoying the sensations familiar to my lost life, the bartender (a petit blonde girl, hair pulled up into a net, her black apron spattered with bits and pieces of foodstuff, stepped my way.

I stood still, watching her come closer until, for one impossible slice of time, we occupied the same space. Her body mingled with mine. She stood within me. Inside my . . . aura? Body? Mind?

In that instant, I knew her, understood her fears, hopes, and dreams. She worried about paying the rent on her small apartment, about the child she left at home with the babysitter, about the future, and her place in it.

I saw her thoughts and memories scattered in small clusters stuffed into the far corners of her mind. Hidden away were the memories of long days spent slogging away at work, cleaning tables, serving the food she couldn't afford to eat, and nights lying alone in bed, wondering about what comes next.

Abandoned by her baby girl's father, she struggles alone, asking herself if this is all there is to life. Just scraping by each day, each week, never getting ahead.

Like her, the girl's mother was discarded first by her father and, then again, by her husband, her baby's father.

With little education beyond high school and few skills, her mother waited tables by day and worked nights in bars. That was her life until, old before her time and worn thin by hopelessness, she grew ill and died.

The girl inside my mind wouldn't accept that for herself; she would not relive her mother's life. She wanted more, a better way of life for her and her child.

Inside the far reaches of her mind, hidden in a dim corner, lived a thought.

The thought was a small thing, a tiny flickering flame blown about and almost extinguished by the fitful winds of doubt.

It whispered to her of education, training, the opportunity for a better job, a fulfilling career, and a better life.

I brushed the thought with my mind, gave it strength, suggested expansion. I felt the idea expand, become bigger, stronger, grow into *more*.

It matured a tiny bit, struggled to become inspiration rather than thought. The young bartender moved on.

The episode, too brief, lasted a bare fraction of a second, yet it seemed as if minutes passed as our bodies touched and our minds intermingled.

Did I alter her destiny, change the outcome of her life in this too-short encounter? If so, did I make it better or, God forbid, worse.

I don't think I'll ever know. It is always possible, but highly doubtful that I will come across the young lady again in some other place and time.

Still, I felt good about the effort. I meant well. I hope that is enough.

I am almost sure it was the right thing to do, although I admit I still have a certain amount of doubt. There is something eerie and unnatural about altering another person's thoughts. Even if it's the tiniest nudge done to help, provide support. I may have overstepped my bounds.

I left the bar the way I had entered, passed through the door, into the street as daylight dwindled, then died, and darkness took its place.

Late into the night, still walking the streets of Denver, I noticed the ghosts among us for the first time.

Their bodies, oddly distorted, with bulbous heads and too-long limbs, were outlined by a pale glow like the fading glimmer of moonlight on the calm, dark waters of a lake.

Their heads always bowed as if looking at the ground, with shoulders slumped; they wandered as I do. They appeared to recognize my presence no more than the living.

There were not many of them; only a tiny handful roamed among the crowds of people. It occurred to me that there should be more, given all the souls that have lived and died over millennia.

They should cover the world, shoulder-to-shoulder; every continent, body of water, landmass should be teeming with them.

Where are they all?

I picked one at random, followed the creature through the alleyways and dark streets. After long minutes of wandering, the ghost (man or woman? I could not tell) ambled into a residential area, walked up a stone pathway to a house, and stood in silence on the small front porch.

Time stretched, minutes passed, each second slower than the last.

Then, the door opened, and a young man stepped out; his dog, a beautiful golden retriever, joined him. The specter straightened a bit, and his pale glow brightened as the dog approached.

The dog whined and sniffed the empty air at the feet of the ghost. It seemed the animal recognized the nearby ethereal presence in the curious way dogs have of sensing things humans can not. The man noticed nothing.

The retriever sniffed again, barked, the sound low and soft in his throat. The ghost leaned forward, his misshapen arms outstretched, seeming to embrace the dog.

His surrounding glow, like cold moonlight, increased again, and, for a brief minute, the creature's ghost-like aura touched the dog.

The dog pranced, front paws cleaving the air, and yipped joyfully. The Golden recognized this shadow-creature, knew the person he once was, perhaps long ago.

The man was smiling too. At the dog's antics, I am sure. If he was aware of the supernatural presence, it was on a much deeper, more profound level. A level his conscious mind could not acknowledge or touch.

"What's up with you tonight, Nikki? Why're you so frisky? C'mon on now, let's take that walk and let you do your business. It's almost bedtime."

The dog sniffed at the spirit one final time, stepped through the eerie glow of the apparition. As he passed through the spirit's shape, his body wriggled with delight. The ghost slumped once again, and his pale aura faded as he winked out of existence.

Was that the end of him? Was he saying his final goodbye? Perhaps he was. Just today, I have seen that there seem too few ghosts for them to remain with us forever.

They must go somewhere. Maybe, after one last taste of love, their spirit, the energy field that holds them here, however briefly, releases them to move on to whatever comes next.

I decided I must look closer at this apparent ending. I knew I had to find and follow another ghost, look closer, determine what happened as the specter's pale halo dimmed and the apparition vanished.

What happens to the ghosts when they fade away? What mystic ability allowed the Golden Retriever to sense a known and loved presence while the human did not? Does love continue? Does it live on even after death takes us away?

I returned to the streets of Denver as the morning sun rose above the treetops, walked the pathways through parks and shopping malls looking for a wandering ghost. I found one or two, here and there, fewer than in the night. Perhaps they have an affinity for the dark.

The ones I noticed seemed to wander without focus or direction. If they had a goal, it was not apparent. I waited.

As the sun progressed towards the western sky, more spirits slowly appeared. I watched, looking for a purpose in their movements.

Pale stars lit the darkling sky. One spirit raised her head as if looking for something. I remember thinking the ghost must be a girl because something about the apparition's movement (not a shuffle but a faintly graceful glide) screamed female inside my brain.

Her movements reminded me of the small steps and swaying hips of young women on the dancefloor.

She spun around, sniffed the air, stiffened like a wild creature sensing prey, then turned from the others.

Heading west, she began the long walk towards faraway houses silhouetted atop the foothills leading to the distant mountains.

The houses, nearly invisible, were dark, angular shapes set against the backdrop of distant stars twinkling in the sky high above the pale horizon.

I followed the spirit creature. She roamed unsteadily from the cracked sidewalk (an ugly, broken thing, lifted, shifted, reset by years of freeze and thaw) to grassy lawns and back again.

In the distance, I watched people walking our way. A group of three teenagers chatted as they strolled homeward. The creature stopped in front of them, spread her arms wide, enveloped them.

As the spirit and the teens merged, the teens fell silent for a second. Then, without prompting, as if the thought entered each of the minds at the same instant, started chattering about a horrible accident, a shattered car, a young friend lost forever.

Tears sparkled in their eyes. The ghost's glow increased as they spoke, her aura bright against the night.

The teens shared recollections, the good times and the bad. Laughter mixed seamlessly with the lingering sadness at the loss of their young companion.

The friend, taken violently from this life, still lived, her memory mingled inextricably within the fond recollections of love and true friendship of those left behind.

They stopped talking and looked at each other as if confused by their sudden thoughts of the girl they lost, wondering why the memories engulfed them. Why here? Why now?

They moved forward, returning to their homeward journey. Walking through the ghost, the pale glow surrounding the entity brightened one last time before beginning to shrink and fade. I moved closer, my attention focused, laser-like, on the spirit.

I opened my mind to what my eyes could not see. The supernatural glow hadn't faded away; it had begun to shrink, squeezing itself ever smaller. The pale halo dwindled almost to invisibility, became a single intense pinprick of energy.

Familiar images filled my mind. I envisioned a giant red star, like Beetlegeuse, falling in upon itself as it becomes a singularity.

The tiny pinpoint of light started to move upward towards the heavens. Instinct took over; purposeful thought left behind, the reasons for action and reaction a thing to be considered later.

I launched my mind towards the escaping bit of energy, followed it with my thoughts. High above, the light, now resembling a miniature star, slowed, stopped.

Beside it, a small patch of sky, circular, faintly outlined in violet, split down the center, opened in a narrow, vertical slit, like the iris of a prowling cat hunting his night-time prey.

Beyond the iris, my mind sensed something new. I opened my thoughts to the limit of their sensitivity, looked deep into the open slit. I glimpsed forked lightenings flashing against a purple night inside the strange aperture.

Each brilliant explosion of light revealed a pulsing globe comprised of uncountable millions of multi-colored threads. Each filament crackled and throbbed with dazzling streams of energy.

The strings were wrapped about each other, inseparable, forming a tight ball that ballooned and then shrank, like the lungs of some gigantic beast. It behaved like a living, breathing organism.

With each breathing cycle, as the orb first grew, then became smaller, the intricate details of the object blurred and faded into indistinct patterns that hurt the eye to observe.

The orb shrunk almost to invisibility, then, in the next moment, reformed, regained its original size. As it grew once again, every detail came into focus, each aspect distinct and well-defined.

The tiniest features became visible as if magnified under a microscope. It seemed like the intricate structure pulsed in and out of existence.

Each unique thread, intricately interwoven with the others, shimmered with brilliant color.

Waves of sparkling energy in metallic golds and silvers, fiery reds, and sunburst yellows flowed along the surface of each strand, going somewhere unknown.

The threads split, then split again, over and over, forming new branches along their length, each new offshoot connected, linked with the old in a never-ending dance, like the continuously growing, infinitely dividing roots of an enormous, immortal tree.

A glimmer of understanding born from studies in the life I once lived - before death came for me (a life now lost to me), grew within my mind.

I recognized what the structure represented. I believed I knew the true nature of the mysterious formation.

It was the face of the many-faceted quantum world, an unsettled place, constantly shifting, creating new worlds from nothing more than probability.

Each new universe was a distinctive reality, as genuine, natural, and stable as the one we've occupied for so long and know so well.

The tiny light I'd been watching gravitated to a single glowing red thread, settled there, then sunk into the thin string, and disappeared from my mind.

The spirit had gone somewhere new, joined a new and different timeline or, perhaps, a brand-new universe, borne of a never before known possibility.

The soul (if that's what it was) had become part of a new life in a subtly different, previously unknown reality.

I understood. The sphere with its many-colored threads represented just the tiniest glimpse of the infinite multiverse, that eternal structure encompassing all possibilities.

Everything that ever was, everything that ever could be or will be, existed within those threads. Every outcome of every decision ever made resulted in the creation of a new universe.

The energy that makes us unique does not disapparate. It migrates to another universe. In the multiverse, all pasts and all possible futures are bound to and inseparable from the eternal now.

It is a timeless place where each of the ghosts had lived before. It is where they will live again, where they've always lived. We live there too.

The spirits of the dead did not die, nor will ours. They continue, we continue, forever.

Perhaps being remembered and loved, the lives they lived and shared embraced in those final moments with family members, friends, even their loving animals, gave them the energy or the release required to leave their old, dead bodies behind and journey onward into a new life, a different reality, and, from there, eternity.

Some may start over, live a new life, never knowing they've lived before. Some may repeat the one so recently completed.

Other souls may transition to a place and time so familiar, so like the one they left, they repeat the life they lost here.

Some force outside myself had offered me a gift. It opened my mind and allowed me to see the multiverse.

It appeared to me as an intricate interweaving of the infinite, simultaneous realities.

There was a reason for the gift. I am sure of this. Can I find it again? Reach out to grasp it from any time and any place?

Time continues its relentless march. How much time has passed since I woke in this strange state of being? I could not be sure.

For me, in this new non-life, the movement of time is like a thick, syrupy mass, no longer constrained by birth at one end and inevitable death at the other; it moves with glacial speed like the slow erosion of the granite mountaintops over eons.

Like others, I moved through time, but it seemed to move so much slower. I did not grow older, become weary, or feel hunger and thirst. I just was.

Time moved on, and I did too. I traveled across the United States, by foot, by car, by train.

I moved through this new world of mine as time crawled past, viewing people, tasting their thoughts, feeling their joys and sorrows.

I did not interfere with the minds of others as I had the first night of this new existence, although the temptation was always with me. I came close more than once.

Often, I became frustrated in my travels. Although I had no physical presence in this world, physical laws continued to constrain my actions.

To take a trip, I had to walk or join living travelers in their cars, cabs, planes, and trains, an invisible presence among them.

Like something out of a science fiction movie, I wanted to visualize a location and instantly transport myself to that place with a simple thought.

I should be able to do this. My presence is unconstrained by time, the need for sustenance, by physical barriers. Why should I be tied to physical conveyances? A question without an answer or with one I could not find.

I visited the universities of America, a silent, invisible presence in study groups, boardrooms, and labs, trying to understand what I am and how I came to be.

I believe the other realities implied in so many quantum equations holds the answers to my many questions. Perhaps they also have the key to the method of travel I so desire.

I have learned little from my continued studies. Later than it should've taken, I realized I needed a time and place for thought, self-examination.

I sensed the answers I was looking for were close, hidden inside myself, and I needed a suitable place to dig within my psyche and root them out.

As I wandered, considering what came next, I often experienced the same odd fulfillment I did that night at the Buckhorn Exchange. Wherever people congregate, food and drink, the glue that binds us, is always present.

I took a seat among young people on the rocky beaches of New England, sampled their thoughts, and smelled the delicious aroma of clam bakes.

Moving south, I tasted the heavenly scent of crab boils on the Louisiana shore.

I've imbibed the steamy fumes of giant steaks roasting over a bed of Mesquite on a Texas grill and savored the scent of homemade tamales in a little border town outside El Paso.

I wanted desperately to gain meaning and purpose concerning this strange new existence. That was the sole intent of my travels and clandestine visits among physicists studying the mysteries of the quantum world. Why am I here? What does it mean, if anything at all?

I found no meaning, no answers. Still, I remained consumed by thoughts of the non-life I live. It must have a purpose I cannot understand. I had so many questions.

How long have I traveled? Months? Years? The world changes slowly.

Considering the small changes I've seen, I put my roaming at no more than three or four years. Too short a time to feel so long.

I have listened to, studied people's minds in my constant journeys, trying to understand my existence.

The time spent has left me with only unanswered questions. I decided to move on, retreat to my grandfather's abandoned cabin high in the Rocky Mountains of Colorado.

Living atop the mountain, I should be lonely. The nearest town is miles away down a rutted dirt trail that, eventually, leads to a two-lane county road.

Only a handful of hunters pass by this cabin. Primarily during the elk hunting season. None stop. Why would they? The place appears empty. It is barren but for my invisible presence.

But the loneliness I expected escaped me. I had only been there three days when the wolf appeared in the meadow on the south side of the cabin.

He seemed to sense my presence. He came to me most evenings as twilight settled on the land. He lay on the porch near my feet, looking directly into my eyes, my soul, and serenaded me with his song.

As the moon rose over the mountain, I leaned close to him and inspected his wild thoughts. I expected little but hunger in my arrogance, perhaps a vague, animalistic sense of the world.

His mind surprised me. The wolf was intelligent in his own, unique way, alive with curiosity and aware of my thoughts sitting side-by-side with his, mingling with them.

There was so much inside that strange mind! His thoughts gave insight and flavor to mine.

He and those like him are more conscious of the living Earth and its many life forms than humans have been since the ancient past when we roamed the savannas of Africa barely more than animals ourselves.

He heard the scampering of the smallest creatures of the forest, smelled their hunger and fear. He was always mindful of his place in this world and only took what he needed for survival.

He never hunted for hunting's sake, knowing life is too precious to be taken away by anything other than necessity and never for pleasure.

I was welcome in his mind.

He became my guide and my teacher. Grabbing my mind with the irresistible teeth of his own, he pulled me into himself. Part of him now, we ran through the night.

Over the days and weeks, he showed me how to open myself, transfer consciousness to other creatures. I have flown with eagles, crawled within the body of a rattlesnake, rutted with the elk.

While inside the tiny minds of beasts, large and small, I lay in wait, ambushed my prey, hid from enemies in small crevices and clumps of brush, safe in the hidden spaces unknown to those who sought to harm me, eat me.

I often thought of the lonesome ghosts I had seen wandering without obvious purpose through the living throngs of humanity.

I started thinking of them as the lost souls that lived short lives of desperation, without hope, love, or companionship, their reason for being unknown and unfulfilled.

They are the left-behinds, abused and discarded, emotionally, physically, by family, circumstance, or life itself.

They died alone in the lonely wastelands of human existence without a single human heart caring about them.

These are the rambling spirits seeking release without success because no one exists to give them that last erg of energy, of desire, needed to set them free.

An idea had begun to grow in my mind. At last, I realized there is some higher purpose in this new existence of mine.

I had learned to inhabit the small lives of living creatures, see the world, indeed, the universe from the perspective of alien minds.

Could I now become part of, look into, and manipulate the quasi-living entity that is the spirit of the departed? Could I introduce them to the entirety of the multiverse?

I knew the time had come to return to the city streets once again. I made my way down the mountain.

After weeks of walking, I found my way back to Denver. Once there, I sought out a quiet place as the evening sky grew dark.

I stood alone in one of the many city parks. Standing there, trying to believe, I opened my mind once again to the multiverse. I visualized that small opening filled with brilliant multi-colored threads of possibility and waited.

Hours passed like minutes, and then, they came. The lost ones who had lived troubled lives, lives without love, without belonging, those who could not find hope or purpose or decency in the life they lived.

They flocked to me, surrounded me, filling the space around me like garbage-gulls at a landfill.

I opened my mind to theirs, showed them the lighted paths to the next world. As one, their ghostly halos shrank to almost nothing.

They climbed the bridge of my mind, leaped through the open doorway, settled onto threads, sunk from sight, and were gone.

Is this who I am now? The reaper of souls? If so, why me?

I have no memory of religious zeal in my previous existence, do not recall granting any theology the absolute truth of the concept of soul, afterlife, heaven, or hell.

I knew only that life was precious, to be savored and shared.

If I exist as a new conduit to what lies beyond, I cannot be the only one. Others like me must exist.

There is simply not enough of me to go around regardless of the enormous amount of time allotted to me in this new way of life.

I may never understand where the ability came from, whether it was a gift from the mythical God in one of his many incarnations around the Earth or the god-like forces imbued in the quantum foam.

I often wonder if the two are not the same, the God-myth somehow emerging from the human need to interpret and accept the quantum realm's unimaginable, seemingly supernatural properties.

Regardless, I will do the job given to me, seek out and aid the wandering spirits needing to move on, but stuck here in their spirit shells, alone in death as in life, with no loved ones to release them.

I will show them the path to their new realities.

And I will look for others like me.

END

Changes

The idea for *Changes* came from researching the concept of planet Earth existing as a single conscious entity encompassing the manifestations of life that inhabit the sphere as well as Earth herself.

That is, the rocks and lava, dirt and dust, oceans and rivers that feed and sustain the creatures living on or within the planet, everything that exists, are an integral part of one massive, living, thinking entity.

I thought about that, wondered what might happen if we humans pissed her off bad enough to shrug off her long sleep and take action to preserve herself.

Changes came from those thoughts.

3

Changes

The world didn't end at 6:00 p.m. on the first day of October 2025.

There was no fire and brimstone. No comet, its orbit disturbed by Planet Nine, escaped the Oort cloud and hurtled towards Earth, ending its long travels in a gigantic fireball as it smacked into the planet, devastating all life on a world once crowded with it.

Neither did an incurable plague, borne of some ancient virus set free by thawing permafrost, scour the Earth, clean it of humankind, life in oceans, forests, and river deltas. The world did not end at all; it just kept chugging along, but it *was* changed. Made into something new. Forever? We still don't know.

I know you remember the day it happened. We all do. The very moment the VOICE first spoke, indelible, is etched into our minds. I thought it a prank at first. I didn't recognize the sound for what it was.

Did you? Did you realize it was the sound of the world-changing? Of course not. None of us did, not at first. I know you think of the words; remember watching as the power mongers of the world vanished before your eyes.

I remember exactly where I was. I will never forget the initial feeling of curiosity and confusion. There was no fear, not at first, just a "what the hell was that" thought echoing around in my brain.

I recall my wife turning to me, a puzzled look on her face, asking, "Rob? What the hell was that? Who said that?"

I believe others all over the world asked each other the same question. "It's a joke," I thought. Some teenage super geek sitting in their dad's basement hacked the TV station.

People everywhere were bewildered by the Event. Fear came into the world later, hours and days after The VOICE (it's always all caps in my mind. I can see it no other way) spoke. Later still, fear diminished, and hope blossomed.

I witnessed the Change as I settled into my favorite armchair, grabbed the remote, and thumbed the TV to life. With a glass of good rye whiskey in hand, I sat, admiring the amber liquid, anticipating the first sip. The evening news broadcast, just starting, recapped the day's events.

There had been a mass shooting (isn't there always) at the Franklin Roosevelt Public School, a combination elementary/middle school just down the road from us. This time, it was close to us, much closer to our home than ever before. Another crazy person or just outright asshole (take your pick) shot a bunch of kids at the middle school. So far, seven known dead and eleven wounded.

I wondered if I might know some of the dead.

The shooter, young and white, a middle-class boy, was the offender. Locked inside room 203 ("Algebra 1," said the announcer. As if that fuckin' mattered.) with a stack of dead bodies, the police negotiations going nowhere fast, he stuck a pistol in his mouth. Smiling, he pulled the trigger, spilling his brains against the black scribbles littering the whiteboard before the police could take him captive.

The police officer at the scene, severely shaken by the violence, was troubled not by the shooting (he had seen others) but by the smile on the boy's face just before the bullet exploded from the muzzle, erasing his grin (and most of his head.)

That boy would've been 14 in another couple of weeks. What fills someone so young with the need to kill people. I don't get it; probably never will.

The officer didn't understand the smile. He couldn't decide if the boy beamed because of all the young lives he took with him or if he was just *that* thrilled to end his own.

In other, slightly less troubling news, the Russians, shaking their fists at the U.S. and the European Union, announced the development of their newest hyper-velocity nuclear weapons, bragged about the devastation they could unleash and the Russian Federation's willingness to use them.

The Russian announcer seemed all too happy to point out that, once launched, no anti-missile system on earth could shoot their new weapon down.

Several countries in the middle east were at each other's throats again. Israel and Syria in an uproar, screaming about incursions, troop movements, and terrorist attacks. The Palestinians were bombing the shit out of the Gaza strip; the Israelis were bombing them right back. Again!

Yemen, Syria, Iran, and Iraq - all were pointing at each other; each country enraged by one or more of its neighbors. All of them threatening to erase the others from the face of the planet.

Near the end of the broadcast, the calmest and, usually, the day's most normal news arrived. The weatherman said there would be, well, weather, rain this time.

Just a typical daily newscast in an increasingly violent world, in other words. Lately, the weather news was my favorite part of the whole evening broadcast. It always presented a welcome bit of low-key routine into my day.

Suddenly the TV screen went blank, flickered a moment, then, immediately afterward, came back to life, offering up the static-filled, snowy screen I remember from my youth.

A big, booming VOICE, sounding like the intermingled vocalization of hundreds of people, male and female, old and young, synchronized in tone and timbre, speaking as one, sprang from the TV.

The VOICE flowed from my iPhone and my wife's tablet at precisely the same moment, the sound reverberating through the room, "We are so tired of your childish ways; this behavior will stop. Now!" it said.

I heard the sound of my network printer whirring to life from down the hall, in my home office, surprising me. It began disgorging page after page.

The printing sped up, continuing until the paper tray was empty. Each page contained one sentence, the identical words uttered from the VOICE on our TV.

Later, over the next day or so, we learned the same message spewed from every television, radio, mobile phone, and computer in the world.

People from rural areas and impoverished countries without such electronic devices or Internet services told journalists of a voice that spoke to them from the sky. Impossibly, each person said they heard the message in their native language.

No matter how the message was delivered, whether spoken or written, each utterance came in the language most familiar to the region.

If the reports are accurate, this seemed to be true even where large groups of different nationalities gathered. Each individual claiming they heard the VOICE in their native tongue.

CNN reported on the message and told their listeners about folks hearing a voice from the sky or received by radios, smartphones, and TVs.

There was even a report of a long-abandoned teletype, connected but forgotten, deep in the lowest level of the Pentagon waking up, chittering away, printing the now universal message.

Simultaneously with the mysterious announcement, heads of state, dictators, demagogues, and prominent religious leaders in every country in the world disappeared. Their closest political partners and co-conspirators vanished alongside them.

They did not gradually fade away like the diminishing light from a setting sun. They did not explode into messy fragments, the bits and pieces of their bloody remains pelting those near them before sinking slowly into the ground. They essentially vanished. Instantaneously.

The North Korean leader (one of a long line of tyrants) surrounded by his generals disappeared in the silent space between two words in the middle of a public speech.

Wherever it was he went, his military leaders went with him. The raised platform where they had once stood was now utterly empty, but for microphones and folding chairs, a silent landscape devoid of life.

The United States Congress disappeared en masse while debating the revocation of a popular health care bill. There one instant, gone the next.

CSPAN viewers thought it was a camera glitch until, many hours later, the cameras still displayed an empty chamber.

The White House stood empty except for a few wandering interns and junior staff; a hollow reminder of power now evaporated. An eerie silence permeated the once busy hallways.

Talking heads from every national news service appeared on television stations around the country. They speculated on the source of the VOICE and the subsequent disappearances. Everyone had an idea about what had happened.

Each religion claimed their God had arrived to wreak retribution on the wicked and reward the faithful. However, the newly appointed speakers for those same religions could not explain why their most prominent leaders had vanished as well. Meanwhile, Christians awaited a resurrection that never came.

UFO enthusiasts insisted benevolent alien caretakers were responsible and waited in glorious anticipation for their unique breed of salvation.

Other UFO believers asserted, just as strongly, it was the beginning of the inevitable alien invasion, anticipating the human enslavement that was sure to follow.

A U.S.-based white supremacist group thought the Jewish Kabbalah were the culprits. The Kabbalah pointed to Satan, reborn into the world.

One theory, briefly popular, surmised the major tech companies' CEOs (Facebook, Intel, Apple, and such) had combined forces in a fierce bid to take over the world.

Their hypothesis: the CEOs combined their technical expertise to develop and deploy an astonishing new weapon to overthrow the Earth's governments. The idea persisted for less than 48 hours, then faded away when it became apparent the tech leaders themselves had vanished along with the politicians.

A variety of recording devices captured many of the mysterious vanishings. Reviews of the films, files, and digital images offered little new information.

CNN, Fox News, and local stations replayed the video of the vanished American Congress incessantly.

Shown in slow motion, the senators and representatives disappeared between one frame and the next. Whatever accessories they held in their hands, papers, pens, tablets drifted to the floor like a multicolored snowfall.

In the first hours after the announcement, the world tried to commit suicide. The U.S., Russian, and Chinese military, leaderless and panicked, all launched nuclear weapons.

ICBMs soared through the thin atmosphere at the edge of space. Missiles dropped from previously unknown and illegal weapons platforms orbiting high above the earth.

Infantry soldiers from opposing factions in Africa, the European Union, Russia, and the Ukraine, North and South Korea, took up their weapons and marched to battle.

In the U.S., Mississippi, Arkansas, South Carolina, Alabama, and Georgia unleashed their National Guard and police forces in a failed effort to revive the old Confederacy.

California passed articles of secession in the early hours of October 2 and posted their guardsmen, police, and local militias at their border.

News broadcasts told the world of impending doom, showed armed soldiers marching in their thousands and missiles arcing over the horizon. Families gathered where they could, spending their last minutes of life together.

All were surprised and relieved when the threat of world wars and civil uprisings ended quickly. None of the nuclear weapons reached their destination.

As they fell from the sky, following preprogrammed paths of destruction, approaching their targets, they too vanished. It was as if a giant, invisible door (mouth?) opened in the sky, swallowing them all.

We watched as they fell through the doorway into nothingness. To the watchers, they vanished in the blink of an eye.

When inspected one frame at a time, news footage showed the projectiles disappearing as they crossed an invisible line in the sky.

Like the sun dropping below the horizon each day, they were gone – erased from reality.

Researchers had no idea where the missiles went. Perhaps they entered another universe, a higher dimension, or simply ceased to be, denied existence by a power we did not understand.

The soldiers of the smoldering wars fared no better. As they raced across battlefields all around the world, raised their weapons, and fired, they vanished, bodily removed from the battle, from life itself.

Nothing remained of the warriors; they flickered like a torch in a brisk wind, then vanished. Their rifles, pistols, grenades, and missile launchers fell to the ground and lay there as if they were child's playthings tossed aside for a later time.

Those soldiers fortunate enough not to have fired their weapons went unharmed. They were relieved to have survived but realizing their peril, they too lay down their arms, surrendering themselves to the invisible force now controlling the world.

Aircraft weapons declined to fire; some planes fell from the sky, others, like the soldiers, were taken from this world.

Once the militaries of earth realized they could not fire a weapon without paying an impossible penalty, their physical (lifeless?) bodies were removed from this reality and sent *elsewhere*, fighting ceased.

Other, smaller events happened. Teams of men roamed the old-growth forests in Alaska, Arkansas, and Oregon, their chainsaws buzzing as they butchered the old trees, withdrew when their saws and other powered equipment failed to start.

The teams, forced to return by logging companies eager for profit, came back with bulldozers and other heavy equipment to push down the trees and drag them out of the wilderness.

As the dozers roared toward the trees, their engines faltered, slowed to a crawl. The drivers of the enormous machines flickered out of existence.

Driverless, the dozers stopped. Their engines idled. The sound of idling diesel motors echoed through the vast forests until their fuel was exhausted. Finally, the engines stopped, and silence filled the woodlands.

Slash and burn efforts in the South American rain forests abruptly stopped when fires refused to ignite. Matches, cigarette lighters, and flame throwers just failed to work.

The men attempting to clear the land gave up and walked away. Similar events happened around the world, the destruction of Earth's resources slowing, grinding to a halt. Coal remained in the ground; old-growth trees continued to live, and the oil and gas wells ceased to pull the precious resources from the earth.

Tomorrow is the anniversary of the Change. One year ago, the VOICE spoke. Influential leaders from industry, world religions, and government disappeared from the earth. If it was *the* God or *a* God, he or she hasn't spoken since.

The citizens of the world have been unusually calm. Perhaps in fear that whatever power did this might return, take us all, erase humanity from life if we misbehave.

Many of the processes of government continue. The remaining employees of the various state and national agencies still go to their jobs, continue to pay the bills, fulfill their duties.

The civil servants of the world's counties are often more efficient and professional without their leaders than they'd ever been with them.

The largest companies struggled the most. As always, they fought to preserve their profits and attempted to come up with new technologies resistant to the Event until, at last, fortunes and will to fight exhausted, they learned the lessons of the unknown force.

For a time, each day or week, someone new would ascend to the position of CEO, attempt to reinvigorate the company. Each, in turn, disappeared, removed from this world, their existence snuffed like pinching the flame from a candle.

Some disappeared in very public places and events; others simply walked into their lavish offices and never walked out.

Their platforms still exist. Facebook is out there. So are Twitter, Instagram, and most others. Their user base has grown much smaller; most of the remaining users seek friends, lovers, or family members that disappeared and will likely never be seen again.

The remaining members of the U.S. government, all lower-level people, haven't attempted to take power, ascend to the top of the political pile.

Although they have, rather timidly, announced new elections for President and Vice President, senators, and representatives.

Remarkably few people have indicated they are interested in the jobs. The ones who have applied seem ... helpful, reasonable, honest. It's almost as if we've rediscovered a long-lost and dimly remembered civility.

I wonder if it will last.

Some question if the government is needed at all. Most agree that some form (the smaller, the better) is necessary to ensure trade, keep the peace, negotiate with other countries, invoke and enforce reasonable laws.

Oddly, much of the world is coping well with the event. North and South Korea appear to be merging into one nation, the people of both countries moving freely across the once forbidding border. No other government has raised their weapons against another or initiated a conflict, not yet. Again, fear?

The most recent theory of the vanishing, proposed by quantum physicists, goes something like this:

We, human beings, create the world, the universe, all that we see and know through some still unidentified quantum process.

Everything we can see or touch, from the chair you are sitting in, the food you eat, even the galaxies with their billions of stars floating through the endless universe, all are shaped by our collective consciousness, by our hopes, desires, and expectations.

A gestalt emerged from the mysterious quantum realm, entangled our collective consciousnesses, gave us the gift of power.

At some point in the recent past, that gestalt (borne of a collective disgust for the shape of the world), the despair, poverty, and hopelessness filling so many lives - emerged full-strength from the depths of our minds.

Driven by anger and shame at those in power, grieving at their inhumanity and contempt for the common man and woman, the will of the decent humans among us merged into a powerful force, a force demanding change. The best of us overcoming the basest.

The voice we all heard was *us*, the combined sound of the peoples of the world screaming, "No more!"

Could that be true? Are we, collectively, the Creator? I like this idea, more than the alien caretaker theory, much more than the Jewish Kabbalah.

Wouldn't it be wonderful if it were true if the power remains and we use it to shape a better world?

Another theory beginning to emerge is that Earth is not just a hunk of real estate suitable for human occupation. It is, instead, a living, sentient being woken from her eons-long slumber by the destructive activity of us, her careless and greedy wardens.

She spoke to us in the voice of the awakened Earth itself. Using the vast powers of her global mind, she stopped humankind's ravaging of her body.

Mother Earth reached out and took from us that singular human trait, the potential for destruction inherent in us all. I find l like that theory too.

Still, the silence following that single announcement from the VOICE bothers me. So does the fact that reports of people disappearing are rare now.

The silence and much-diminished disappearances concern me. Was the Event a brief, spectacular occurrence, designed to get our attention before leaving us to choose who and what we will be?

I believe the day will come when we understand if either theory is correct if the power we all witnessed is still with us.

Humans are limited in their ability to sustain fear. We, instead, adapt to it. We forget because forgetting is a magnificent, although dangerous, coping mechanism.

Someday, a year from now, ten years from now, someone will pick up a gun and take a shot at their neighbor.

Perhaps a young man or woman of ill intent will rise to power somewhere in the world and attempt to rebuild their armies, reignite wars with old enemies.

If the gestalt's power has diminished, faded over time, its elemental force broken by the peace and calmness that followed the VOICE, that man or woman will succeed. We can expect the same result if, instead, the living Earth has returned to her long sleep.

Perhaps it will be as simple as one man taking the life of a person of different color or religion than them and surviving, staying in this world to strike again.

We will know if the world will survive or perish when that day comes. I have this terrible vision of the earth writhing in anguish, overcome by greed, prejudice, and hatred as the peoples of the planet return to the old, not yet forgotten ways, and once again march towards oblivion.

We may never know which theory, if any, is correct. Does it matter if it was a human gestalt or Mother Earth, reaching out with the VOICE, telling us to wake up, stop and think about the damage we have done to the world and each other?

Either way, for a too-short time, we have been better than we were before. I hope whatever or whoever spanked our butts over inexcusable behavior stays with us until we learn the lessons he/she/it offered. Perhaps we humans can leave our turbulent childhood behind and become adults, custodians of Earth, and each other.

END

Do Over

The next story, *Do Over*, came from daydreams of a better time and place. This story, born of fear, frustration, and desire, is a result, I am sure, of a dark time in my life.

It is, in part, a story of the Great Recession and the damage it did to many in the United States and around the world.

The Great Recession changed my life. Why? It's like this:

I took my first real job other than chores around the house, my first paying job, in the spring of 1958, the summer before my tenth birthday.

I delivered the Arkansas Gazette by bicycle to about 150 residents of a tiny town in Arkansas.

It was not a job that I wanted but one my mother requested I take over from my younger brother.

Her request came the day after she discovered that, after collecting the newspaper fees each Saturday morning, and, his pockets heavy and jingling with coins, he'd stop at the local Ben Franklin and spend the afternoon buying cap guns, comic books, and candy until the supply of money was exhausted.

That's how my life as a working, productive member of society began and continued without interruption for the next 50 years.

That life came to an end on October 24, 2008, when the Great Recession kicked into high gear and I was 'downsized' out of a job. I became one of the unemployed for the first time in my life.

The following story is a result of thinking about a dismal future following too many months of unemployment. A long fruitless search for work most likely triggered the idea.

I was in a downward spiral of self-doubt and the emotional and financial devastation wrought by the great recession, all accompanied by the genuine fear I might never find work again.

The basic idea for *Do Over* came to me in the middle of one restless night as I struggled to find sleep. My thoughts consumed by how much life sucked after close to eighteen months of unemployment.

I had just one more week before the bank was due to foreclose on my home. At the last possible instant, I was saved by an old offering a good job.

The idea I had was about how one might escape an impossible situation by returning to a carefree childhood and doing life over again.

. I filled in the blank spots left by the dream-like concept but kept the idea of stepping backward in time into a different, better time.

This is *Do Over:*

4

Do Over

Two months before his strange disappearance Wayne Humphrey lived through the darkest days of his life.

Fearing the future and what it might hold, despair grew stronger every day. Hope faded, leached away bit by bit, like memories of a long-ago childhood eaten away by time.

The Great Recession stripped away the pieces of his life one thin slice at a time, like a vulture ripping flesh from the corpse of fresh roadkill. The financial collapse took his livelihood, his confidence, his courage.

His life was lying on the chopping block, out of work, out of luck, the bank on his ass about foreclosure; he was desperate for a job.

Wayne hitchhiked the forty-mile stretch from his home to Denver. He was looking for work; anything that might feed his family and save his home would do.

It wasn't the first time he made the trip. Wayne had thumbed his way to Denver a dozen times or more over the past year and a half.

He hoped for a different outcome this time, but his faith in success, muted by previous failures, was fragile and easily broken.

Wayne feared, once again, he would find nothing. Turned out he was right about that.

After two days of meetings with recruiters, a couple of too-brief phone interviews, and a night on a friend's couch, he started the long trek home.

As he walked the roadside, thumb out, hoping for a ride, he wondered (not for the first time) where it would all end. He started to think he might never work again.

By the time he caught a ride home, the late afternoon sun was sitting on the horizon. Dreading the coming conversation with his wife, hating to tell her he had found nothing, he opened the front door.

As he stepped inside, a sensation of emptiness rolled over him like a cresting wave. Something was very wrong. He tried but couldn't understand the feeling at first.

Everything looked the same. The furniture still in place, kitchen radio softly playing the oldies station. Still, the sensation of wrongness persisted, sharper than ever. Like a lead ball, fear sat heavy in his belly and ate at his psyche.

His home felt abandoned. The hollow echo of his footsteps followed him as he crossed the hardwood floor. An empty silence hovered about the place like midnight in a museum. Or cemetery.

He found the envelope, his name printed in heavy, block letters, on the kitchen table but did not open it.

He sat at the table, stared at the letter like it was a dangerous animal that might jump up and bite him, and waited while the Autumn darkness slowly filled the room. Minutes (or hours) later, he flipped on a light, studied the envelope.

Sure he already had an idea what the letter said, he opened the envelope and read. Marcy hadn't bothered to take it easy on him or herself. She had opened her soul in a few words written carefully on a single square of pale blue parchment.

"Wayne,

By the time you read this, I'll be gone. I'm sorry. I'm just not strong enough to live this way, watching you die a little bit every day.

You don't need to know where I'm going. Wherever I go, I'll be better off, and you'll be better off without me. It's been over a year since you lost your job, and I can't stand watching you blame yourself.

Let the house go. Quit fighting the inevitable. Go somewhere new and start over. I wish I could come with you, but the past months have broken me, broken our marriage. Maybe our bond was always too fragile to survive but never tested until now.

Take care of yourself, and please, please know I loved you as best I could for as long as I was able.

Marcy"

Wayne tried to make sense of the words. He couldn't. They might as well have been written in an ancient language, found in a hidden crypt buried for centuries, and never deciphered.

He went to the fridge, pulled out a beer, wished he had something a lot stronger. Sometime later, head spinning, eyes blurry with tears, he re-read the note, then read it again, one last time, each reading as painful as the one before.

He might've been home sooner, caught her before she left if he had driven his old F-150, but there was no gas in the tank. He couldn't spare the money to buy more.

The little cash sitting inside his front pocket was his emergency reserve for food. The next unemployment check wasn't coming his way for another two weeks.

He believed he'd done his best, searched on the Internet every day until he ran out of money to make the payments and his provider shut the connection down. They'd lost the Internet and cable TV stations a couple of months back. "The cell phone will go next," he thought.

Marcy didn't understand; it wasn't her fault; she couldn't. The whole world was in the toilet these days. She had never worked, didn't have to. Wayne always made good money and took care of everything; until he didn't.

He crumpled the note, tossed it in the trash, walked to the living room, and pulled out an old photo album. Collapsing into the La-Z-Boy, he opened his favorite album, the one labeled 1955.

Memories echoed through his mind as he flipped through the pages, "God, those were good times," he thought.

The album, a time machine into his past, packed with old black and white photos, filled him with warmth and desire.

He scanned them all; he and his best friend, John, sitting in the shade of the giant cottonwood, playing in the dirt; his brother fishing at the Charlestown lake the day he won first prize for catching the biggest fish.

He looked at the picture of that ugly fir he and his sister cut for Christmas, must've been '55 or '56.

The damned old tree's branches poked out in all directions, without any symmetry at all but the smile on their faces told a different story. There was pride, even joy, in what they'd done. They were happy.

It occurred to Wayne that being happy was a familiar feeling back then. What happened to that? Where did that feeling go? He wondered if he could ever find peace and happiness again.

Those days, so long ago, were simpler, safer, better. Somewhere along the way, all that changed. By the time the financial crisis hit, there was nothing left but work and worry.

Even weekends were mainly about resting for the coming work week rather than enjoying life and laughing with family and friends.

It finally sunk in. Marcy was gone. She ran out of patience, understanding, or, more likely, hope and had to go.

Wayne didn't blame her. The last eighteen months had been hell for her. Bill collectors calling every day, stretching food, trying to get by until the next unemployment check came in, watching him struggle with the inability to provide.

Wayne figured she couldn't face another week of Hamburger Helper, living without TV or any kind of entertainment at all. There'd been no date night, no going out for dinner or a movie in months.

The thought rolled through his mind, "life changes, cruel events occur, emotions unravel, and everything falls apart." He thought he understood.

Fear and uncertainty pushed him to spend too many nights sitting alone at their kitchen table. While he worked over the bills, worried about food, and wondered what came next. A wall, too high to climb, slowly grew between them.

He could've spent those nights in bed with Marcy, holding her, telling her everything would turn out alright if he had just a bit more time.

He wondered where she might have gone and who might've gone along with her. "Probably home to her daddy," he thought.

Her brother, Eli, undoubtedly came to get her, he thought. Didn't matter. She was gone now, out there somewhere chasing whatever passed for happiness these days

He pulled the picture of John and him out of the album, studied the photo, worn and faded with age, for a minute before sticking it in his shirt pocket.

Thinking "happiness isn't a myth, something chased but never found. This picture proves it", he snatched up the album and walked out the door.

His thoughts turned to his dad's tiny hunting cabin. Some of his best memories were made right there inside that cabin and roaming the surrounding forest.

He and his dad had trekked through about a million miles of the woodland, climbing hills, fishing in the nearby lake, hunting squirrels.

He smiled at the memories and the warm feelings that accompanied them. Then, his decision made; he locked the house, tucked the keys under the front mat, and walked away.

Thumb out, hoping for a ride as far up the mountain and into the backwoods as he could get; he thought, "I'll go up there, be by myself for a bit.

If I can find a way back to the happiness I knew as a kid, maybe I'll find it there." Wayne understood he might be looking for something that no longer existed.

Two months later, Sheriff Bobby Crenshaw parked his truck and stepped out into the predawn November morning.

The brutal cold, driven by a strong east wind, seeped through his heavy sheepskin overcoat and chilled his blood.

Turning east, towards Mount William's, he caught a brief glimpse of the morning sun as it fought, and failed, to break through the bruised clouds hanging low over the craggy peaks of the San Juan's.

He stepped to the sidewalk just outside his office, stopped, lifted his head to the sky. He looked at the heavy, purple clouds and sniffed the morning air. The taste of snow lingered in the wind. Bobby wondered how bad the coming storm might be.

Crenshaw walked into his office thinking how badly he needed the storm to hold off a bit. A man was missing. Discovering what had happened, finding him if possible, was his most important job.

That man, his friend, Wayne Humphrey, had disappeared three days before. So far, nothing about the case made sense.

Witness statements all agreed. Wayne went missing right before last call at the local drinker's paradise, the Grizzly Rose Bar and Grill.

His tiny town held a couple of quiet, family-style pubs, but the Rose was home base for the roughnecks working the oil and natural gas fields that littered the nearby landscape.

Those folks worked hard and played harder during their short breaks away from the oil fields.

Late in the night, only a handful of people remained in the bar. Earlier in the evening, the place would have been packed. The sheriff thought he caught a break with fewer people to interview. More people always meant more stories, all different.

Bobby questioned the people who were at the Rose the night Wayne vanished. Most, busy at the pool tables or on the dance floor, didn't notice anything. The few that did told what they remembered.

Only two witnesses were right with Wayne and saw what happened up close and personal. Rik Stephens (who most people called Big Rik) and David Root. Bobby knew them both, had been friends with them for years.

Both told a strange hard to belive version of events. Still, Bobby only had their story to go on. He decided to start the day reviewing the sworn statements before heading out to the site of the disappearing act one last time.

He liked being the sheriff; the job appealed to him when the city offered him the job. He accepted the badge thinking small-town police work would be tedious but fulfilling.

Coming across a situation as odd as this never entered his mind. He never once thought the work would be lonely either. As it turned out, he picked up the strangest case of his long career around the same time loneliness crept into his life.

"Life doesn't often turn out the way a man thinks' he mumbled to himself. "God's honest truth is I'm almost never bored but always lonely."

Anna, his wife of close to forty years, had died one month shy of two years earlier. Cancer hit her hard and fast. Anna died only six weeks after the diagnosis.

Most of the time, he spent the days alone in his office. He missed his dead wife most at the end of each day, nearing the time to lock the door and go home.

The two years seemed far longer. "Time is like a rubber band that stretches out and grows thin, especially when a man's too much alone," he thought.

Often, he didn't lock up at all. Anna's memory haunted his home, leaving the place too empty of life and too full of memories to bear.

Since her passing, he lived in the office more than his small two-bedroom house. The old leather couch tucked away in the far corner of the office suited him better than his bed as often as not.

The office had been his workplace ever since old sheriff Murphy retired eighteen years earlier and Bobby took over the job.

Murphy grew up in the town, held the title of sheriff for almost thirty years. It took a while for the place to get used to his leaving, but this was Bobby's town now. He walked the streets every day. Greeting the business owners as they swept the walkways or wiped clean the window fronts.

They smiled and waved when he walked past them, headed to or from the office. Talking with the townsfolk was a large part of his job, and he spent much of each day chatting with the people he knew so well.

He shook their hands, asked how they were, talked to them about the weather, crops, their kids, and high school ball games.

He was always there, doing his job, keeping them safe. Spending his time with them, knowing their names, their fears, and concerns was important. He cared about the people of the town, and they cared about him in return.

Bobby stood at his office window and glanced out over his town, little more than a small village, but the residents liked to think the place larger than it was.

Looking around the office, he realized how much he loved the place and the work he did there. Everything about the old office was unique.

The look of the place, the sense of history and permanence, even the aroma marked it as different, distinctive. Responsibility and permanence hovered about the office, almost like a physical presence.

Modeled after the typical sheriff's buildings of an earlier era, the office looked much like any other might've during the middle years of the nineteenth century.

It was easy to imagine the holding cells filled with a handful of Butch Cassidy's Wild Bunch or one of the James boys, sitting on their bunks waiting for the circuit judge to come around, listen to their stories, and hand out whatever justice he thought necessary.

He loved the texture and strength of the knotty pine walls and dusty hardwood floors. He always felt the weight of the years when he entered the building. As often as not, he wondered if he was as much a relic as the office.

Friday and Saturday nights, he usually took a drive down to the Grizzly Rose to spend a few minutes chatting with the doorman and barkeeps. Some nights he spent more time breaking up fights and arresting drunks than talking.

The rowdy crowd of roughnecks, youngsters from nearby townships, and a handful of vacationers looking for excitement needed a place to do a little drinking, get a bit wild. The Grizzly filled the need.

This morning any wandering passerby might mistake Crenshaw for a statue if they happened to glance his way.

He stood at the plate glass window covering the front wall of the sheriff's office. Motionless, his thick, calloused hand gripping the window frame, head bowed in thought, his mind wandering through the events at the Grizzly Rose three days before.

Silent minutes later, he shook himself as though waking from a long, troubled dream, raised his head, and stared out at Main Street, his hometown, Morsetown, Colorado.

Thick grey-blue clouds dropped from the cold November sky. The dense clouds a sure sign of heavy snow coming and likely to arrive soon.

The streetlights still cast a pearly luminescence on the roadside at 5:30 in the morning. Not a single person strolled along the sidewalks, and no cars cruised the streets. In the eerie light of early dawn, the town appeared abandoned.

Remnants of late October leaves drifted in the wind, tumbled down the street, and over empty sidewalks cracked and buckled by years of winter freeze and spring thaw. "Christ," he thought, "looks like a damned ghost town."

Tasking a deep, exasperated sigh, Bobby turned back to his desk and rifled through the small stack of notes and interview transcripts littering the desktop.

He rubbed his calloused hand through short, iron-grey hair as he thought. "Goddamn it! Here I am. Sixty-nine years old, over forty years a cop, and never seen anything like this. Gonna retire in less than a month, and now I get this crazy shit," he mumbled to himself

He thought, "How can I write this crap up? People know me. Hell, they like me. They're my friends and neighbors. When the story gets out, they're gonna think I lost my mind."

The phone rang—the loud, piercing sound shattering the deep quiet of the office. Bobby jumped, reached for the phone, knocked over his coffee mug. He managed, somehow, to sound calm as he answered, "Sheriff Crenshaw."

"Hey Bobby, Dave Root here. Got your message. You need to talk to Big Rik and me again?"

"Yeah, Dave. One more time."

"Well, that old truck of Rik's broke down again. Damned Fords anyway! I gotta go pick him up. We'll be there soon as we can, shouldn't be long."

"Thanks, Dave. Won't take long. I promise to keep it short. We need to go over what happened at the Grizzly last Friday one last time."

"Damn Bobby, what's left to say?"

"Come on, Dave. Don't give me any trouble. Mary Lynn over at the Gazette called three times yesterday, so did the mayor. I can't keep telling them I need another day.

Just drag your butt in here, tell me your story one more time. After that, I'll be done with you 'till the next time you find yourself fallin'down drunk, and I gotta drag you out'a the Grizzly. Then it'll be a night in the cell for you and another hundred-dollar fine."

"Jesus, Bobby! You don't gotta get all uppity on me."

"Sorry, Dave. I got to tell this crazy story to Mary Lynn and the mayor and write the damned report. I need to make sure I have the facts right. Help me out here."

"I know you do, but it is what it is, Bobby. The story won't change, not even a little bit. Look, I'll grab Rik, see you in about ten minutes, could be a little more."

Crenshaw thought Dave might've slammed the receiver down pretty hard. He didn't blame the man.

"Probably as tired of the whole mess as I am," he mumbled to himself.

He wandered over to the Mr. Coffee machine in the corner and started a fresh pot. He drank too much of the stuff. Always had.

"Twenty-five years being a cop for the Army, then another eighteen right here in this office and always with a cup in my hand. This stuff will kill me someday," he thought.

Anna pestered him to cut back for years, and he had. By the time the malignancy took her life, he was down to only two or three early morning cups.

After her passing, how much he drank didn't seem to matter so much anymore, so he quickly fell back to the old ways. These days he always has a steaming cup in his hand, sunup to sundown.

The coffee had almost finished making, the old Mr. Coffee machine gurgling and spitting as the brew finished. Bobby picked his battered mug up off the floor, inspected for new cracks and chips, and started to pour a cup when the door swung open.

Dave Root stepped in, followed by Big Rik Stephens. "You boys want a cup," he asked.

"Sure thing, Sheriff, Sir," said Rik.

Bobby chuckled, "Sir, my ass. You never called me Sir in your life."

"Only tryin' to be respectful of the law, Bobby," Rik smiled.

"I hate to trouble you boys, but I need to go over this one more time before I do the report. Have a seat."

Dave and Rik took their coffee and settled into the stiff oaken chairs opposite Bobby.

"Damn, Bobby, buy some cushions for these things. It's like sittin' on a brick," Dave complained.

"Talk to the mayor. He owns the budget in this town, and I ain't high on his list of priorities this year. Not any year, for that matter. Nothing much happens in this town that requires a budget bump for the sheriff."

Dave shook his head, "Well, something sure happened here a couple'a days ago, didn't it now."

"Yeah, well, I guess you're right about that. Let's get down to it."

"Ready when you are."

"Dave, you called me that night. Told me Wayne had gone missing. Sounded like you'd been drinking. The truth is you weren't making any sense at all.

At first, I thought you meant someone took him, like a kidnapping. After a minute or two, I realized that didn't make any sense at all. The man didn't have shit, not a pot to piss in as my momma would'a said."

"I know what you're thinking. You believe I was drunk, but you're wrong about that, Bobby. I'd only had one before he disappeared. I planned on having two or three more that night. They closed the place down and locked the doors when you showed up, or I might've.

A beer or three seemed the right thing to do after Wayne up and disappeared. Sitting with us, right next to the jukebox. I saw it with my own eyes. He was right in front of me one second, gone the next. Never seen anything like that, sure as hell don't want to again."

"You two meet Wayne at the bar pretty regular, didn't you?"

"For a time, we did. Wayne, Rik, and me, we'd meet down at the Grizzly every week or so.

That sorta died away the last year or so. Possibly a bit more. Got so we only met up with him about once every couple'a months, sometimes might've been three.

Wayne couldn't manage more than that. You remember he lost his job, right? Been more than a year since the man had a job.

No job, no money, no prospects; that hit him real hard, and he stopped coming by, stopped seeing anyone. Got so we practically had to go by and drag him out'a the house."

"Yeah," Rik said, "he kinda gave up. On everything. I think Wayne applied for over a hundred jobs, every job opening he found from here to Denver.

There were no jobs to be had anywhere, nothing for him at all. Not a damned thing. Dave and I met up with him about three months ago, and he mentioned they might take his house. Foreclosure was coming at him fast. Only had a week or two before it was a done deal. That's what he said."

"Yeah, I heard, and I checked it out. The mortgage company had plans to take back the house next month. Right before Christmas. Christmas! Christ, what a fuckin' holiday present. Did he talk about that much?"

"Nah, not really," Dave said. "got so he only wanted to talk about was being a kid. Thought he might somehow find a way to start life over from the beginning. Wondered if things would come out different."

"Start over? How the hell could he do something like that?"

"Hell, Bobby, I don't know. He was different those days, not himself. I sometimes thought he might cry, and he might have, but, fuck, men don't cry. Not in front of other men, they don't.

Wayne talked about being young again, the scent of magnolias and mimosa when they bloom in the spring.

Sometimes talked about playing on the school playground or watching the hummingbirds drink from the morning glories that grew around his Mom's front porch.

He talked about how different things were when he was growin' up, safer, simpler, better. Fuckin' Mayberry, RFD, is what it sounded like; some perfect little podunk town in the south, I think."

Crenshaw nodded, "Arkansas, Charleston, Arkansas. His sister told me when I called. Had to tell her Wayne had gone missing and ask if she'd seen him or might have any idea where he would be."

Rik muttered, "Seen him? Seen him! Goddamn it, Bobby, she ain't seen him. Nobody's gonna see him ever again. I'm telling you he's gone.

I was sitting next to him, looking right at him, when he just up and vanished. One second, he was talking to me, and the next, he turned all misty, was like looking at him through the thick smoke from a campfire, and then he was gone. Just fuckin' gone.

She ain't never gonna see him again and you ain't gonna find him. He went somewhere, Bobby. Somewhere *else*. He left this miserable fuckin' life for somewhere better."

"Damn it, Rik. That isn't possible. Here we are, and here we stay until we die. For better or worse, this life is what we've got."

"Damn it, Bobby! You think I don't understand that? On Friday, down at the bar, he told me he had discovered a way, said he figured out how to do it."

"What way? There isn't a way. You can't go back. There are no do-overs, not now, not in this world."

"I understand that. I know you believe what you say. The way he told it, he had learned to dream. That's what he called it -dreaming.

Not with his mind but with his heart. Said he needed to gather all those lost memories, all the special times, back when life was good. Gather them and hold them in his mind, all at one time.

Not only think about the events but relive them, feel the passion, fear, sadness again. Wayne said he needed to understand all that stuff down deep inside his soul, remember everything that happened, the time, the place, and, most important, what it felt like, relive the emotions of the time.

He said to think about 'em hard. Hard enough to feel the breeze on his face, the June sun on his back, the morning dew brush against his legs, and smell the spring flowers beginning to bloom.

Said if he did that, got everything perfect, some kinda door would open, and he could, you know, step right through. Sounded bat shit crazy to me. But what the hell could I say to him? The poor miserable fuck had lost everything; he had nothing left."

Dave stood, walked to the window, looked out at the empty streets, stuck his hands in his pockets. He cleared his throat. When he spoke, his voice husky and cracked, he said, "Go on, Rik, tell him the rest."

Rik was quiet, lost in thought for a minute, then said, "Listen up, Bobby, me and Dave, we didn't say everything about that night, the way things played out.

Don't write! Just listen.

<u>Me, Dave, and Wayne, we're sittin' at the table back in the corner near that beat-up old jukebox. Patsy Cline's singing Crazy and Wayne's sipping on a beer and holding this old picture.</u>

It's a picture of two boys, little kids around five or six years old. They're sitting in the dirt under this old, giant cottonwood tree. The bark's peelin' off in great chunks, and they're playing around with the stuff, makin' buildings, coulda' been houses or barns. Somethin' like that.

They had little toy cars or somethin', was hard to see what they were holding.

Wayne flipped that picture over and showed me the back. "The Gold Dust Twins, 1955" was scribbled at the bottom.

The ink was old, starting to fade away. Didn't matter; I could make out what it said, no problem."

Dave whispered, "He said the picture was of him and his best friend, John, the summer of '55. Then he started talkin' about how good things used to be. Back before Vietnam, Kent State, the Watergate crap, and Clinton's goddamned blow job. In the Oval Office, for Christ's sake.

He said all that crap robbed us of our innocence, and the inexcusable criminals running the banks along with the greedy Wall Street assholes stole our hope."

"He stared at the picture and talked about things that are long gone or maybe never were, and, suddenly, he started to fade.

Swear to God, Bobby, I was lookin' right at him, hell, man, looking right *through* him, was the weirdest damned thing I ever saw. He kept on looking at the picture and smiling and then . . . then he just disappeared. Like smoke in the wind, he was gone.

You can say we went to take a piss if you want. You can tell everyone Wayne finally gave up and walked away into the night.

The truth is, Rik and me, we know different. We watched him go. And you know what? Right before he disappeared, when we could still see him, shit, see straight *through* him, I swear I heard little kids laughing and saw a playground, like it was far off in the distance.

Might'a been one of those mirage things, but I don't believe that for a minute. I could see a bunch of kids out there, back off in the distance. There were a couple'a boys in overalls hangin' upside-down on the monkey bars.

A bell was ringing like fuckin' recess was over or something. And, I swear, for a second or two, the thick, sweet scent of mimosa filled the air."

Dave turned from the window, faced his friend, the Sheriff, reached into his pocket, and said, "Write what you want, Bobby, we'll sign it, even swear to it."

He pulled a single, waxy white flower from his pocket, held it out to Crenshaw, and said, "but you keep this. Keep it and think about it. I found the flower on the floor under Wayne's stool, picked it up, and stuffed it in my coat pocket before you showed up."

Dave dropped the blossom on Bobby's desk. A limp relic of itself, the flower was wilted. The pale white petals had begun to yellow with dark brown spots creeping around the edges.

Dave gathered Rik with a look; they both stood and walked to the door. Bobby picked up the flower, held it close, inhaled the fragile, lemony fragrance of Magnolia, and mumbled to himself, "Those boys may be right.

They went to take a leak, and while they were gone, Wayne walked away into the night. Left for another place, a better, safer place, somewhere he might start over. Yeah, that sounds about right."

END

The H.O.A.

This next story was fun. It shouldn't have been. We, the whole world, were just coming out of the Great Recession; most everyone was miserable.

They didn't care about silly stories. They cared about the next mortgage payment and the next meal. I know! I lived that life myself.

I started writing as a venting exercise. I was in the middle of an argument with my Home Owners Association. It wasn't pretty!

I understand that some HOAs might be good, even beneficial. Mine was a nightmare assembly of busybodies and know-it-alls. All I can say is, when it came time for me to move, finding a new home without an HOA was at the top of my list.

I pictured all the HOA members as secret Nazis. They might not have been, but they sure acted the part.

The Nazi caricature morphed into stranger creatures, the story evolved into something I never expected, and I ended up with the weird little story you get next.

Welcome to *The HOA*.

5

The H.O.A.

My son believes the whole world might come crashing down around us at any time. He's not a full-blown prepper, but he leans in that direction. He often tells me, "You know the world's gonna blow itself up – one way or the other - but you try not to think about it. It's a little like dying. You realize death is coming for you someday, but you push that thought away. Until the dark man with the scythe is standing right there next to you."

He might be right. Someone, a Kim Jong Un or Putin or Trump, could lose their goddamned minds, push the big red button and erase us from the planet in a nuclear fireball.

Or some asshole terrorist (or an inattentive scientist at the US Army Medical Research Institute of Infectious Diseases) sitting in his basement lab could set the world afire playing around with a virus, an Ebola or superflu, and kill the world.

Those scenarios are more likely than an alien invasion or another Chicxulub style comet smacking into the Earth; you know the one, the great ball of ice and rock that wiped out the dinosaurs.

I always knew that shit was possible because I have always understood the unlimited idiocy of the human mind. I never once thought I might be the one to set us on the path to the end.

Just so you know, it wasn't my fault. I didn't plan it. It just happened.

It all started with painting the house. My Home Owners Association sent me an official letter. It said I had to paint my house. They didn't say why I needed to paint but were adamant I complete the work in ten days or pay a fine and still must paint the damned house.

It's a long story. The house needed painting; I understood that. I had seen the paint slowly fading, beginning to peel, and spent about a month looking at different paint schemes.

The HOA didn't like my color choices (a pale yellow with white trim reminiscent of the New England shore); I didn't like theirs (pale browns and paler grays).

Unwilling to stand against them and fight the good fight, I went to the nearest paint store to pick up paint chips from their approved list.

The store couldn't help; they didn't make the approved colors any longer, had removed them from their inventory ten years or more before.

As much as I disliked the idea, I needed to talk with the HOA pricks. I'm not being the asshole here. I had dealt with the HOA before. They reminded me of the Soup Nazi from that old Seinfeld episode. Only harsher.

With the day of the fine was drawing closer, I telephoned the HOA and suggested they might be more selective in their color choices.

They suggested I shut up and do as I was told. I couldn't put it off any longer; it was time to visit their offices.

A few days later, I learned they were more and less than I thought. I arrived on a Wednesday afternoon around 2:00 p.m., walked into the office, and asked to speak to someone about their house painting criteria.

The receptionist was a small girl, almost childlike, with the most amazing eyes, emerald green, somewhat almond-shaped.

"A man could get lost in eyes like those," I thought. I put on my best smile and said, "I need to talk with someone about your approved paint pallet.

"Please take a seat. I'll tell Mr. Barguest you are here. He's in a conference with the board. Would you like coffee, perhaps a bottle of water, while you wait?"

"No, no, I'm fine."

She turned to enter a long hallway that led, I presumed, to the conference room. I waited, checked the time on the office clock, picked up a magazine (The HOA and You), glanced at the wall clock again, and waited some more.

I waited over an hour for her to return, but she never did. These people were really beginning to piss me off.

Angry and out of patience, I decided it was time for me to go see where the hell everyone was and what was taking so long.

I didn't think it would hurt anything to walk down that hall and peek into the first conference room I found. I was wrong about that.

I walked down the long hallway. There were no offices, only the hallway leading to a single, ornate wooden door.

The dim hallway lighting got a little darker with each step. By the time I reached the door, it was like walking through the woods at twilight on a cold winter evening.

I tapped gently on the door – nothing. I knocked louder – still nothing. So, I eased the door open and stepped inside.

This was no conference room. It had no conference table, no chairs, and no people. An enormous leafless tree stood alone in the center of the room; flickering orange light seeped from globes randomly hung about the lower branches.

I glanced upwards, wondering how tall the tree was. I couldn't see the top. It was lost in a cloudy haze drifting across the deep purple of a deep twilight sky. Far higher than any ceiling could reach, a thousand stars flickered through the gaps in the clouds

Bursts of lightning flashed in the unreachable darkness above. Strange creatures, impossible to name, soared and flittered amongst the highest branches.

Perhaps they were some unusual breed of bat or nighthawk or something utterly, disturbingly different altogether.

A second nearby tree had been cut through the center about three feet off the ground, leaving a flat, table-like surface.

A tiny naked girl, not more than a foot tall from head to toe, hovered above that surface.

Her incredible magnificence was carried aloft by fluttering, iridescent butterfly wings glowing in all the colors of a rainbow.

Her body glimmered in the soft golden hues of a perfect summer day. She was a breathtakingly beautiful creature. More so than anything I'd ever seen in my life.

She did not settle gradually to the tabled surface as I thought she might but stretched and grew until she was more than twice as tall, and her toes touched the surface. She tiptoed to the edge of the table-like top and sat looking up at the soft, orange lights.

Sitting in amongst the gnarled and twisted roots of that huge old tree was the ugliest fuckin' thing I had ever seen.

As large as a brown bear, covered in a thick mat of dark hair, long pointed ears, and a mouth filled with crooked yellow teeth. A pale white snake lay in his lap.

I scanned the area, trying to find the far wall. "It must be there," I thought. After all, the damned building is only so big, but I couldn't find it.

A small grove of skeletal trees stood where it should have been. Scattered among the trees were creatures from dreams, storybooks, and nightmares.

A unicorn with a golden spiral horn stood in the distance, partly shrouded by a light, roiling fog. Next to the unicorn, I saw what appeared to be a small, silver-scaled dragon breathing small patches of fire that lit the area around him. His fiery breath illuminated all manner of creatures, great and small.

A slender old man stood by the dragon's side, his long ash-gray hair hanging to his shoulders.

He held a crooked wooden staff with a jagged, glowing rock at the top in his right hand. I immediately thought of Merlin, but the old man was no more than five feet tall. I expected Merlin to be tall and regal.

Standing in a patch of tall grass, close to him, stood a small creature, half man half goat and, behind him, among the small, twisted trees, what could only be a centaur.

Clearly, somewhere between the waiting area and the conference room, I had lost my goddamned mind. Either that or my HOA was populated not by humans but by evil goblins, beautiful winged faeries, and the ugliest members of the brown dwarf clan.

I looked back at the beautiful winged girl. She'd hopped down from the table and approached the ugly thing sitting at the base of the tree. She knelt before him and reached to pet the pale snake. She stoked it with gentle fingers before leaning forward to kiss it.

The ugly bear-like didn't notice the girl but stared towards where the wall should be but wasn't. Instead, I swear to God, moving pictures shimmered in a heavy mist.

It was a movie playing without a projector of any kind. The bear-creature watched Disney's Sleeping Beauty and roared his approval each time Maleficent appeared.

I turned away from the winged girl and noticed, for the first time, a book lying on the tabletop tree stump. I stepped to the stump and peered down at the book. I touched the cover and felt the oldness of its rich, dark leather, creased with age.

At the top of the ancient cover was a globe of the Earth showing familiar but strangely altered continents. As I stared at the sphere, it started to spin very slowly; the eastern coast of the Americas vanished to be replaced by the Atlantic.

A large island appeared in the middle of the Atlantic ocean, a land that did not exist in my world.

To the north, the English Isles and Ireland, both bigger than I remembered, were surrounded by several smaller islands I didn't recognize. The globe continued to spin.

Beneath the spinning globe, markings that resembled text in some old, forgotten language, runes perhaps, were carved into the cover. I gazed at the markings, and they began to shift and change, growing more and more familiar until the words became clear.

The markings said:

Decree of the Aos Si

I opened the book and read the first page:

These are the words of the Elder Aos Si, the ancient Sidhe of the time before time.

Since time long forgot we have watched the coming of the creature that is Man. We have observed as he makes the old gods dwindle away to be forever lost in the mists of forgotten memory.

Our worlds have been taken away by the human tinkerers, those without spirit, without the sight.

They are without the magicks in their soul. Humans are beings that wriggle their fingers to make things with their hands and not with the powers of the mind; the ones that cannot see or touch or taste the sinuous lines of Power that flow through all things and can be turned and twisted into the shapes of good or evil.

Their One God has made small the old Gods and left them to vanish from this world and the next.

Comes now the time of the Sidhe, the Goblin Kings, the Witches and Warlocks of old, the Spirit Kings of the trees and stones and flowing waters. Comes now the Black Magicks and White Magicks of the fey folk. Comes now the time to regain the World that Was.

Comes now the time to unleash the Magiks of old and break the human hold on this the sister world of our Home.

We shall strip them of their many glittering trinkets, make them cease their workings, and fall silent.

We shall take from them as they once took from us; leave them leading the horse, pulling the cart, living with only the light of the candle that casts our shadows on their wall. Metal birds will not fly, metal carriages will not walk.

We will take from their imagination the small few that see faintly the glimmering of the World that Was and leave them in the darkness that flows about them, strip the sight from their eyes.

They shall be left as they were at the beginning of their days, insignificant beings without Power that fall to their knees in our presence and pray to Old Gods for deliverance.

When the sister world is once more clean and fresh, we shall reclaim our Home and make it green again.

Dryads will nourish the trees, and Water Gods will return to the streams and rivers, the God of the East Winds shall gather together his brothers of the North, South, and Westerly breezes. They shall refresh our home and spread again to the sister World.

Once again, Woden, Queen Mab, Myrddin (who is called Merlin), and their ilk shall walk the World that Was and make it again the World that Is.

Never again shall the humans despoil this world, our Home, and take it from us.

So say the Aos Si. So say the Gods of Old.

I glanced around the room that was not a room but a hidden world. The eyes of all that lived in that place gazed back at me. The winged girl once again hovered above the table. She floated towards me, growing taller as she approached.

She drifted before my eyes, touched my lips with tiny fingers, and I felt warmth, love, beauty, and fear when she smiled.

Her tiny teeth were needle-sharp. She touched my cheek with her lips, so red, so hot, so soft, and pointed to the flat surface of the tree stump.

She leaned towards the tabletop, stretched out a finger, and began to draw letters. Where she touched the stump, the wood smoked and turned black. Again, she glanced towards me, and pointed to the word written on the table.

run

So, I ran. The outer office no longer looked like the typical, everyday office I had left. The TV was dark, the screen cracked, smoke curled from the side of the computer, and the florescent lights sputtered and flickered, sparks littering the floor.

I should have told someone. I did not. Who would believe? I should have found a way to fight for our technological world. I did not.

I am not sure I cared about the world, only myself and my family, so I kept running. I took my wife and daughter and left that afternoon.

I don't remember if I closed the door to my home or left it to hang open as I drove away. Sometimes that bothers me.

We made a run for our cabin high in the Rocky Mountains. We've lived here for nearly six years now. I won't tell you where, but I will say the village is small and remote. We have no TV, no cell phones, no Internet.

I grow what food I can in the short mountain summers and always look to the fields and thank them for their bounty.

I fish in the rivers, hunt in the forest, and stop to thank the waters and tree-covered slopes for feeding my family.

I don't know for sure if anyone or anything hears my words, but, so far, our lives are prosperous and untroubled.

Perhaps the streams, fields, and trees listen and appreciate the thanks.

We produce our electricity. Most of it is made using solar panels, but we have a growing amount coming from water wheels we set in the rushing mountain streams. Still, electricity or not, I taught myself to make candles, you know, for when the time comes, if it does.

An old woman named Emma prints our newsletter once a month. I think she makes the ink herself, but I don't know how she does it.

Life is smaller and slower here, so Emma doesn't need to print much. Most news spreads quickly around the village by conversation, person to person.

Strangers pass through from time to time. Some walk up the mountain trails. Others come on horseback, and a few come in cars that shudder and clatter and smoke their way up the mountain.

We listen to their stories. They tell of things breaking, failing, and never working again. Gremlins, maybe, ghosts in the machines or invisible (to us) strings of magical energy unleashed to kill the mechanical beasts. They tell of strange creatures that roam the dark nights.

There is a war between our machines and the magic I unleashed on the world the day I opened the door in the H.O.A.

The war is not won and may not be for a long, long time. But I believe it is truly being fought, a struggle between what is, what was, and what is yet to come. I don't know who will win.

Sometimes in the darkest hours of the night, I sit on my porch, cigarette in one hand, coffee in the other, and think about the dream or vision or warning given to me back in the HOA office that was not an office but a portal to some strange world.

It is vivid in my mind. Sometimes, I glimpse the beautiful, glowing lady fluttering through the trees as I gaze into the forest. I think she smiles.

I think we may need to move soon. Too many folks have found their way to our mountain home as they try to escape the cities.

From the stories the new folks tell, we know the cities and small villages deterioration continues to accelerate as technology fails.

It sounds like the cities are dangerous places. Outlaws bands roam those places, fight over food and water.

I think it is only a matter of time before the food is gone and the outlaws head our way.

I mean, come on, when you think about it, even the small cities are dependent on technology. For power, for water, for all for their food, everything the city dwellers need to stay alive.

Our most recent visitor, Old Abraham Ledbetter, gave us a pretty fair idea of how bad things had become when he came to us.

He ran from Colorado Springs and the outlaw bands (they call themselves The Tribes) who control what's left of the food markets. He found his way to our small village here in the mountains just a month or so ago.

Crazy old fucker came up the beat-up, washboard dirt road riding an ancient mule. God only knows where he found the sickly old beast.

That mule was damned near as grey and wrinkled as Abraham. Abe was sick and dehydrated. Looked like he hadn't had any food or water in days.

The mule appeared to be in as bad a condition as Abe, gaunt, unsteady, his ribs showing conspicuously. He was puffing and blowing and making an ungodly racket, his braying loud enough to shake the windows.

Abe can't remember where he found the mule or much else about the last two or three weeks of his trip. He was lucky to he found our cabin. Or perhaps luck didn't have anything to do with it.

That mule found his way along the narrow path to our place, stopped right beside our old redwood porch, and stood still, braying at the house until we came out.

For a second or two, I thought I glimpsed the little winged girl sitting between his ears.

I might've been wrong about that. I didn't see her when I got to the mule but, then again, the fairy girl seems to come and go, appear then suddenly disappear as she wishes.

I was barely in time to catch old Abe as he fell from the ugly old creature's back.

Abe and the mule found their way to our door only minutes after me and Becca made it home from our last run down the mountain.

We went looking for all the things we didn't pick up before we abandoned our home on the outskirts of Colorado Springs the same day I met the little golden fairy girl and all her friends back at the offices of the Home Owners Association.

It was our last run. I was afraid the old RAM pickup might not start this time around. It, too, is feeling whatever energies (magic?) the strange creatures from the HOA let loose on the world. At first, it coughed and sputtered and shook like a rabid dog.

I was about to quit trying when the winged lady popped into existence, floating above the hood. She pointed at the truck, and it coughed into life.

I wish the little bitch would talk to me, so I might have some idea of what she expects me to do. She never does, of course. She smiled at me for a second or two, and, poof, she was gone again.

God help me, I decided to trust her, and we made a run to the nearest supermarket and Home Depot we could find, both deserted by now with much of their products stolen away.

Not much was left, but we grabbed what we found, canned foods, flour, and sugar from the market, tools (axes, hammers, a couple of saws, and boxes of nails) from the depot.

On the way home, we came across a partially burned-out Walmart. Most everything worth a shit was gone, no guns at all, but we found ammo for the 12-gauge shotgun and 22 rifles. We found a Coleman camp stove, a compound bow, lots of arrows, and almost four dozen small propane bottles for the Coleman.

We got lucky there. A wall had collapsed and covered the stuff in rubble. Becca found what appeared to be the handle of an axe.

We found most of the other stuff when we pulled the piles of concrete, drywall, and insulation away.

We made it back up the mountain just as the RAM started coughing up smoke and, finally, died as the dirt road to our little house petered out at the end of the driveway.

I think my little butterfly-winged friend had something to do with the timing of that.

Old Abe remembers the city (or what's left of it), and he remembers the tribes. It took almost a week tending him, feeding him on a thin broth at first, and working our way up to a hearty stew; rabbit and squirrel with a few bits of potato and carrot we had saved back.

He was feverish the first couple of nights, kept waking up rambling about taking care of Homer. It was his third day with us before I figured out Homer was that damned old mule.

Abe figured Homer saved his life, and I guess he did. In his condition, I'm certain Abe wouldn't have made it to us on his own, not making the long, steep climb up the mountain.

I told Abe I took the time to brush Homer and tie him to a tree out in the grasslands near our place, then made sure he had plenty of water to go with the meadow grass. I checked on him every day.

Damned if he doesn't look better, a bit younger all the time. The mule is old. I expect he will never look great, but he is as healthy as his old bones will get, I think.

Once I told Abe I was taking care of his mule, his health improved. He got better faster. On his sixth night with us, he was finally able to sit out on the porch, a cup of hot, black coffee in hand, and tell us a bit about the troubles in the city.

"It's bad down there," he said. "The power failed in fits and starts at first but was entirely gone in a little over a month.

The water system kept working for a lot longer, but eventually, that failed too. A couple of the larger tribes took over the reservoirs and traded water for food and other essentials.

Food was the biggest problem. Corner stores and supermarkets were such a big part of our daily lives most people took eating for granted.

In only a few days, power failures killed off all the frozen food, especially the meats.

Canned foods, dried beans, and rice lasted much longer, and a lot of that stuff was still left on shelves and, sometimes, floors of abandoned stores. Still, a hell of a lot of people remained, and they all needed food. I figured the store supplies would disappear pretty damned fast."

I could picture what he meant. Colorado Springs held about 400,000 people when this all started. Abe figures there might be a quarter of that now, maybe less, probably a lot less.

Abe continued his story, "People disappeared from the cities by the hundreds after the first couple of weeks and in the thousands by the end of the second or, maybe, third month.

By then, the tribes started to form and looted most of the gun shops and other stores keeping weapons of any kind and started staking out their territories. We talked late into the night as Abe let his story dribble out in bits and pieces.

It's almost funny if you think about it. All the big markets, King Soopers, Super Walmart's, Safeways are now headquarters for one tribe or the other.

Those places, easy to defend, stockpiled with plenty of canned foods, dry beans, and rice, were perfect for survival or trade. But they never traded. They simply killed anyone trying to get to the food and bottled water supplies."

Turns out that's how Abe lost his wife. I didn't think he would make it through that part of his tale for a while there.

They got jumped by a gang of thugs as they left a Circle K, not more than a block away from their home, over a six-pack of bottled water.

"Members of one of the biggest, meanest tribes, call themselves The Wild Bunch, caught us.

Them people never said a word, never tried to talk to Jenny and me," he said, "just jumped us as we started to leave the store.

It was just goin' on dark when we slipped out the main door. They grabbed Jenny first. She tried to pull away, and some dirty little shit, a kid not more than twelve or thirteen, shot her in the face with a sawed-off shotgun.

I tried to get to her, but this enormous, ugly biker guy smacked me in the head with a stick or baseball bat, somethin' like that.

I woke up sometime later, don't know how long it was, figured they left me for dead, or I wouldn't of woke at all.

Jenny was gone on to the next world by the time I woke. The gang took the time to strip the little store of damn near everything it had, anything of value anyway.

The stupid bastards even took all the money in the till. Not sure why. Money is worthless these days."

Abe told us he rummaged around the remnants in the store until he found a couple of leftover bottles of water and some Twinkies.

He could do nothing for Jenny but sit by her side, hold her cold hand and say his goodbyes. As the moon started coming up, he stood and started stumbling his way out of the city.

The old man cried for a long time then. I sat with him as he mourned his Jenny. There was nothing else I could do.

I thought about his story and his life. I'd asked once before why he and Jenny stayed so long in the city.

The answer was simple. It was the life they knew, and their home was out on the edge of town where things we a bit safer.

Many of the small neighbor stores had been left alone for a long time. I imagine that was because there was so much more available in the bigger stores, like the strip malls and megastores down near the center of town.

As the supermarkets started to run out of food, the tribes began expanding their territory. Abe and Jenny waited too long, felt safe in their small town. They weren't.

After a long time, Abe looked up, blew his nose on his shirt sleeve, and said, "that's all done now. Thanks for watching after me – and Homer."

"Where the hell did you find that old mule anyway, Abe?"

"Didn't. He found me. I walked for most of two days, was outside the city headed towards the mountains, aimin' for Pike's Peak.

Don't ask why. I don't rightly know; it felt like the right way to go. I had hardly any water or food and was mighty afraid of checkin' out another store.

Think I must'a passed out and fell somewhere along the way. All I remember is walkin' towards the Peak.

Next thing I knew, ole Homer was pokin' at me with his nose. I got to my feet, and we walked a bit, side by side, 'till I come across a big old pine tree laying across a ditch, killed off by the beetles, I guess, and used that to climb up on his back. Next thing I remember is wakin' up in your little house."

I let Abe wander into the house to sleep but sat on my porch for a long time. One thing was clear to both Abe and me. Our food was about gone. The bits and pieces the tribes were always fighting over would soon be gone as well.

Someday they would come this way, looking for everything they didn't have. A few stragglers (or scouts) at first, more of them later, coming more often as finding food got harder. We needed to get out and find a safer place.

I thought on it for a while that night and figured, come morning, I'd tell Becca and Abe I needed to leave them for a bit.

My grandmother Rose owned a cabin, thirty miles as the crow flies, from our village but much farther by road and mountain trails. It had been in the family for damn near a hundred years.

I needed to find my way to it and see if it was safe for us or if someone had found it and taken it for themselves. I didn't think so. It was hard to find, stuck way back in the deep woods with an almost invisible trail to the place.

When I was a kid, we backpacked our way to the cabin or went horseback. It wasn't an easy trek, but I needed to be sure. I told Abe I would have to take Homer if it was OK with him and if he thought the old mule could make the trip.

"That mule is stronger than you think and stubborn enough to outlive us all. He'll take you there and bring you back safe,"; the old man said.

So, I filled my backpack with what I needed, grabbed the 30-30 and a handful of shells, and said my goodbyes. I told Becca to keep the 12-gauge loaded and by her side till I got back.

Becca's a strong woman. She'll take care of Abe and our daughter, Holly. Holly is only six but wise beyond her years. She will keep her eyes open, stand guard with her mom.

Homer was where I left him, looking better than ever, stomping at the ground all full of piss and vinegar. When I got right up close to him, there was the little golden-skinned girl, beautiful wings all aflutter, a smile on her tiny face, sitting between his ears.

I guess she's going with me this time. I pray to God she's here to help and doesn't get me killed.

Hopefully, I'll find out why she helps me while the world falls apart. Abe wants to come too. I tried to talk him out of it, but he's a stubborn old man, and he won the argument. I hope letting him come isn't a mistake.

Homer, good old Abraham Ledbetter, the little golden fairy (or whatever the hell she is), and I have crept through the dense forest of the Rocky Mountains eastern slope, thick with pine, aspen, western hemlock, and juniper, for most of a week now.

We stick to trails where cars and trucks (if any still work) can't follow. Abe's convinced the tribes, and the people they chase out of the cities, are coming up the mountain in greater numbers than ever. I haven't seen 'em myself, but I trust Abe.

After all, it has been six years since an ancient doorway to the worlds of myth and magic swung wide in the offices of my Home Owners Association.

When the door opened, creatures known only through the old legends and folk tales burst forth, and magic poured back into our mundane world. The effect was localized but immediate. It was the beginning of the end of the world we knew.

Things electric were affected most. They sputtered and failed in fits and starts. I fled Colorado Springs the day the Door (yeah, with a capital D – after all, it did open to a different world) was flung open, took my wife, Becca, and newborn daughter, Holly, and ran for the high mountains.

We lived there, gathering the few who found their way to our cabin into a new village and new way of life, a life lived in the old way without electric power.

We learned to grow some necessary foods, hunt for meat, make candles, and do all the things required to live a simple life.

Abe came to us a couple of months ago, hanging onto the back of Homer, an ancient old mule who'd found him passed out on the side of the road and nudged him back to life.

Homer brought Abe right to our porch. Then stopped and made enough noise to raise the dead. Braying his loudest until we came outside. As soon as we stepped out, he quit his braying and has not made a sound since.

We had other visitors before Abe. Lost and lonely wanderers haunted by the things they had seen as the world's technology crumbled and fell. But Abe was able to tell us the most about the happenings in the world beyond our village.

Abe stayed in his home on the outermost edges of Colorado Springs through the long years as the magic and the creatures set free spread across the land.

All because I ran out of patience and opened the door to what I thought was an office. It was a doorway all right, but one to a world only known to me in fairytales from my childhood.

Abe told me he had listened to the radio and picked up TV stations as far east as St. Louis and west to Arizona and New Mexico.

At first, the stations played on much as they always did but, by the end, as fewer and fewer stations continued to operate, no more music came from the little boxes in every home, only a few newscasts, talking heads trying to make sense of what was happening.

His TV was reduced to white lines and static by the end of the second year. By the third, the radio fell silent as the last of the television stations went off the air for good.

Before they died, the stations told stories of giants, centaurs, and chimera walking the streets, of griffins, dragons, the cockatrice gliding through the night skies.

Their last broadcasts told listeners stories of everything electric failing, of ghosts and goblins, fairies and unicorns, Grimms' Fairy Tales come to life.

People ran from the cities or stayed and died. Some from starvation as the tribes in the Springs and their counterparts elsewhere took control of every available source of food.

Others died from the violence done by the tribes, and still others from unwise and failed attempts to attack the newfound creatures in the night.

The tribes and their like were the worst of it, vicious gangs roaming the darks streets of cities, taking what they would from all those weaker than they, robbing and killing, staking their claim on the new world.

The supplies in the bigger cities lasted much longer than I thought, likely due to the massive exodus into the countryside but, too quickly, not enough was left to sustain the much-reduced population.

Then the smaller villages and towns started to fall. Even the farming communities that had briefly come back to life as city folk rushed to find a way to grow food to feed their families.

Some of the farms evolved into giant communes and fared well for a time until the tribe's food stores dwindled away to nothing or almost nothing. They moved into the smaller communities when they needed more than they could find in the decimated super-stores and came hunting.

The day came when Abe's wife, Jenny, lost her life over a single container of bottled water found in a burned-out old corner market. After her death, he walked, alone, out of the city into foothills looking for peace or hope or, perhaps, something he couldn't name.

We were careful on our trip from my small cabin to the log home once owned by my grandmother. We took forest roads and log trails unknown to most, one eye always looking for strangers the might be wandering the forest. We saw none.

Abe rode Homer much of the time, and the little fairy girl always rode sitting between the ears of the old mule. We talked of the world as it once was and how much it had changed during short breaks from our journey and as we rested during the late evening meal.

The fairy girl stayed with us during the day but vanished into the dark each night as we settled down for the evening meal and a much-needed rest. She never spoke but appeared content to be with us.

I often sat alone with the dying embers of our fire after Abe was asleep and wondered where she was and why she stayed with us. The first time I met her, she gave me two gifts, a kiss on my cheek and a chance to run from a place that was, yet was not an HOA office.

After we settled in the high mountains, I would see her sometimes, flitting from tree to tree, watching the cabin. I'm sure she has a reason to be here, but I cannot figure out why. I keep hoping the time will come when she will communicate. Time will tell.

We settled into a clearing in the mixed woodland of fir, Pine, and Aspen here at the end of our eighth day of travel. Eight days but only sixty-five miles or so as the crow flies. We saw no one during our travels.

We were wise to stay off primary roads and well-known trails or, perhaps, we were lucky. Even when we crossed high above the pass overlooking I-70, there were no people, only abandoned cars spread along the freeway; lifeless shells like the empty husks of cicadas hanging off a tree, stretching into the distance, as far as we could see.

I wondered where all those folks went and if they had lived or died. The missing people puzzled us.

No bodies were strewn about, rotting in the vehicles or lying on the roadway. The few we found looked to have been killed by bullets, arrows, or beaten with hammers, sticks, or baseball bats. The signature of death by the tribes or, sadly, each other.

Most people were just gone, vanished, disappeared, leaving no bodies and no clues to where they went or what happened.

Tomorrow we will reach the log home built so many years ago by my grandparents. It is just over the next rise and a few miles down into a small valley.

Abe sleeps while I watch the last embers of our fire die away and wonder if the old home place still stands as it has for generations. I pray it's in decent shape, ready to become our next home.

As the fire died away to nothing, I rolled into my blanket and let sleep take me away.

She called my name while I slept.

"John Roberts Silver. Speak with me."

It seemed I was still caught up in a dream when I opened my eyes. The fairy girl sat cross-legged on my chest, her sea-green eyes softly glowing.

Her butterfly wings fluttered, opening and closing with each breath. She glowed with a pale light reminding me of the fireflies I chased as a child.

She sat and gazed at me in all her naked glory, hair, like long strands of fine-spun gold and silver, spilled across her shoulders and tumbled down her back, eyes like green fire, soft, succulent lips mouthing words I heard in my mind but not with my ears. Her lips did not move, but I heard her speak again; "John Roberts Silver. Come! Speak with me."

I was surprised. I didn't know the little Queen (she had to Queen of something, right?) could speak aloud. So, I figured, "why not?" and started to say something.

Before I said a word, she reached out, moving faster than anything I'd ever seen, and placed a finger on my lips.

I thought her the most beautiful creature ever to live. With her colorful butterfly wings, glow-in-the-dark body, and hypnotic eyes, she made all the Victoria's Secret models in the world look like the old, used-up bag ladies.

She was the antithesis of those poor unfortunates you hear about hanging out in city parks, dollar store parking lots, homeless shelters, and the dark alleyways of the most miserable cities of the world.

As these thoughts raced through my mind, she smiled. When she smiled, the sound of crystal bells rang through my mind, and I realized it was her laughter. The sound of those tiny bells fell away, and her voice rang in my mind, "what is a bag lady?"

I spent a couple of days in downtown Manhattan once upon a time and, over the years, had seen about a thousand episodes of CSI (back when TV's still worked).

An image of a wrinkled old lady dressed in filthy rags pushing a loaded cart came to mind. The fairy girl, saddened and embarrassed by my mental picture, glared at me, shook her head, and looked away.

I opened my mouth to speak. She held up her hand in the universal "stop" gesture, then turned and pointed towards Abe across the dying fire pit. A fine mist of glowing green energy fell across his sleeping figure.

I started to protest when she spoke aloud for the first time; "Your friend is not harmed. He will sleep and hear nothing while we talk of the past that was and the future that may be and why I came to be with you."

"Start at the beginning," I said. "Who are you? Do you have a name?"

"You know who I am, John Silver, but you've forgotten much. Your kind has always known about my kind. My name cannot be said in any human language. You may call me Belle."

"My kind? What the hell do you mean by my kind?"

"You are The Dark Man; he who is often called The Night Stranger, or Night Walker. The natives who lived in this land before white colonists came in their boats to rape the land called you and those who lived before you, He Who Walks with the Stars.

Your father was a Night Walker, as was your father's father, and so on back to the beginning of time. As far back as the days before human writing existed, when history was just a story passed down, mother to daughter, through the spoken word."

"What in God's name are you talking about?"

"Stories of you and those like you have been told through the generations, for thousands of your years. Some think you are searchers for someone or some*thing*.

Others think you are stealers of small children and still others think you come to steal souls in the darkest hours of the night. There are other theories. All of them are, of course, wrong."

"Lady, you have me confused with someone else. I am, or was, a computer technician, for God's sake."

"You are more. It is the fault of the Aos Si that your legacy is forgotten. When humans came to this land to kill us, the original inhabitants, pollute the waters we drink and the air we breathe, we left you alone to see who you would become.

Humans grew in number faster than we imagined. Like rabbits, you spread across the land, spreading your filth with you.

You changed the world, made it worse, infected it with sickness and death. Suddenly, there were too many of you.

We closed the paths leading to our world, isolated ourselves from you. We erected unseen barriers to prevent Humans from finding and trying to use the old pathways. Then we withdrew from your world."

John's mind was spinning. "Stop," he said. "Please stop."

The fairy girl stopped talking. She stared at John, puzzled.

"I get it," John said. "Humans did bad things, so you guys left the world, somehow. How does any of that concern me? Why do you stay near me?"

"We didn't leave *our* world, John Silver; we left *your* world. Most of us did. Our worlds have always touched each other. They are sewn together along many paths in many places.

They always have been. People of both worlds walked freely between the two for eons. Until it became necessary for us to close the paths. We thought we had made ourselves safe from the destruction of your people. We were wrong."

"So, there are two worlds? Each touching the other?

"There are many worlds. They all touch in many places. The place you call Ireland is littered with them. But they exist throughout your world and ours and the many other worlds that live side-by-side.

Where worlds touch, a path between them always exists. All your many peoples tell legends about the pathways. They have called them by different names; thresholds, gateways, and crossroads are the most common."

"Belle, help me understand. When I opened the door, the one I thought was a conference room, I opened a path between our worlds?"

"You did. It did not matter that it was you. We were all gathered to open the pathways once again. It was time to fight."

"Fight? Us? Why?"

"Our worlds are tied together closer than we knew. Your people damaged your world so severely it was beginning to die.

The coming death created vibrations that crossed over to our world. We learned the worlds must both live or die as one. We entered your world to stop the destruction and save ourselves."

"I still don't know why you came to me. I am only a man. I have no power to help. I know nothing about what can be done or how to do it."

"John Silver, you are the Nightwalker. You are of both worlds. In a time long forgotten, your ancestors passed the power of the Nightwalker from father to son, mother to daughter for generations.

When we closed the paths, the passing of power and knowledge stopped flowing and, over the long years, who you are, what you do was forgotten."

"I keep saying I am a computer tech, and you keep saying I am something else, something different. How do you know you're right?"

"There is one of us who has an affinity for you and those like you. You are not alone; others exist. We set the Searcher loose in your world many of your years ago. His only purpose was the seek out you and those others like you.

Some of your people may have noticed the strange little man. Leaning on his oaken staff, hobbling along the streets of the world's cities in the dark heart of the night, sometime after the last call at the local tavern but before the first hint of the new dawn touches the far horizon.

If you are one of those who are awake in the long hours of the night, it's possible you spotted him quick-stepping from one street corner to the next, slipping silently from one puddle of shadow to the next.

Perhaps you would've seen and instantly forgotten, the street lights dim as if power was being sucked from them as he brushed past.

If you are a person of the daytime, you would see him not at all. The sun does not like him. He does not like the sun.

It was while sitting in the darkest corner of a pub in Dublin, the Molly Maguire just off Green Street, drinking a pint of stout he had felt the birth pains the day you were born."

"Belle, my world is dying right now, right this minute. And your "people" are doing the killing. While you sit here telling me stories."

Her eyes flashed neon green. "My people have killed no one!"

"Explain all the empty cities if you can, the strange creatures roaming the land, the cars sitting empty on the highways. Where are those people if they're not dead and gone?"

"The creatures that crossed over from our hidden realm do no harm, bring no danger to you and yours. They exist to bring the magic back into this world. They do not hurt living beings. Your people are gone but not dead.

They are between worlds. Neither dead nor alive, neither awake nor asleep. They are in stasis waiting for you or one like you to open the door to their new world."

"You opened the doors, not me."

"It took all the energy of our most powerful to reopen the door to your world. We need you to find in yourself the power given to you at birth, the force which opens the door to new worlds. That is where your people will live."

"Why? Why send them somewhere else?"

"Humans almost destroyed this world. With your help, we will move them to new homes. They will go in smaller numbers, a few million to each world. You will open many gateways."

"So, you're giving them a chance to start over, learn new ways?"

"Exactly. Now you sleep and think about my words."

With that, she vanished, and I sat alone pondering her words long into the night. She was wrong about people dying.

Possibly she and her kind took no lives, but humans killed some of our own in our fear and distress. The tribes killed more than a few.

If I had the power to open these doors the fairy girl spoke of, I needed to recover the skill and do whatever I had to do. First, though, I would move my family to the cabin and tell them the story Belle told me. Maybe Belle would sit on my shoulder and assure them the tale was true.

Then I would do what I could to open new worlds. Someone else would need to teach the people of those worlds how to live and prosper without destroying their new home.

END

Outsider

This next story is for my little brother, Rodney Gene Mannon. He was the best man I ever knew, and he died too young. No, he didn't leave this life the way I tell it in this story (it is, after all, a work of fiction), but he might have had things played out a little differently than they did.

Childhood sexual abuse is alive and well in America and the larger world as well. Rodney and I lived it, and that basic fact served as the seed that made this story possible.

Much of what you are about to read is true. Just as much is pure fiction. You'll get that (in spades) as the book progresses. The idea of another, better life waiting "out there" somewhere, is a constant of most religions, but this is not a book about any religion or, really, the afterlife.

It is a story about escape and hope. This tale's escape scenario twists some of the stranger ideas of quantum physics into unrecognizable shapes before it wanders off into the wilderness of science fiction. Writing the story was a work of love for the brother who is gone. It was also a healing exercise for me.

You should know that the dreams detailed in this story are real, as genuine as the abuse we suffered. I still have horrible nightmares that chase me out of bed, a dark shape hovering over me.

The monster in my mind vanishes as soon as I am fully awake, but my battered knees hurt from falling out of bed far too often.

The good dreams, the ones about life in another world where my abuser never existed, come to me less often, but they **do** come, and I look forward to their arrival.

Maybe I should have dedicated the story to every child ever abused, but Rodney is the one I know, the one I miss.

Parts of the story will disturb you, as they should. But, maybe other parts will show you the glimmer of hope that lives in us all.

Now, I give you *Outsider:*

6

Outsider

I am a haunted man and have been for years. Spirits of the dead are not to blame; my memories of childhood sexual abuse are. I wish those memories would go away, die a miserable death, and lie, moldering, in some forgotten grave for eternity.

That's like wishing on the evening star for an impossible dream; world peace, immortality, or universal acceptance in an intolerant world.

Still, it's a wish I make every day.

Haunted, look it up; to haunt or be haunted: You'll find things like "to visit often," "to recur frequently and spontaneously," or "to stay around or persist," or (and this is my favorite) "to appear habitually as a ghost."

Take your pick of any of those definitions. Any of them, all of them, apply to me. How did this come to be?

A boy can be changed forever, eternally damaged by one person, one horrible act. It happened to me.

So, yes, I am haunted, stalked in the depths of the night by horrible nightmares. The dreams wake me, sweaty and shaking at that time of night many people call the witching hour.

The witching hour sounds like a terrible and frightening time when ghosts and demons come for your soul. Oddly, no one agrees on exactly when the witching hour occurs.

The exact time it comes is unimportant. That it comes at all is. My nightmares come when they will but often appear in the deepest hours of the night when darkness reigns.

I've had bad dreams for almost my whole life. I wake up sweating and trembling in the dark, too frightened to breathe. A monstrous shadow-creature looms over the bed, reaching for me, his long, thin claws like daggers.

The beast has no mouth I can see, but I know it's there. It is open, gaping wide with jagged teeth dripping slimy, poisoned drool.

As the sharp claws close around my head, I scream in my sleep. The thunderous screams echo in my head but emerge from my mouth as soft whimpers.

There is not enough air in my lungs for an earth-shaking shriek, the sound rattling the walls, waking the neighbors. Fear has constricted my throat and paralyzed my vocal cords. The demons who haunt me muffle the sounds of my terror.

No one ever hears my cries.

I have other, less terrifying, nightmares that raid my sleep. Those come courtesy of Vietnam and PTSD. The doctor down at the Veterans Administration gave me pills to stop those.

I'm supposed to take those pills every night, but I don't. Some nights, not enough, but some, I have a different sort of dream, a wonderful one that fills me with wonder and hope. I'm afraid the medicine will stop these good dreams that sometimes visit me.

When the pleasant ones come, they offset the terror of the recurring nightmares. Those good dreams are the ones that take me to a different life in another world. They sustain me and give me hope.

More and more often, I remember how my dreams (both the good and the bad) first came to me. They are relics of my tortured youth that move closer as old age creeps up on me. They hover about me like a dark cloud.

I'm 75 now. Like most older folks, I have a handful of ailments to bother me, some more serious than others. Sooner than I'd like, not today or tomorrow, not even next year, but soon enough, my time on Earth will expire.

Even ten more years leave me closer to the end than the beginning. I may have ten (or more) left in me, but I am well aware of what awaits me somewhere down the road. Life's timer will drift lower, then lower still, until its skinny black needle flutters into the red zone before finally dropping to zero.

Lately, I lie in bed at night as images of the past flicker, like silent movies, across the screen of my mind. Scenes from long ago yesteryears stutter and jump as the memories drift through the synapses of my brain. My subconscious conjures the clatter of an old eight-millimeter projector.

I have to smile as I imagine a smoke-filled basement room, a white sheet hung against the far wall, the projector's light flickering like dim lightening.

The movie in my mind rolls on, and I enter the world that was as I step into the year and the events that removed me from the world and left me isolated and alone.

The summer of 1955 comes alive in my thoughts. That was the year my young, still-forming mind first witnessed and recognized the changing of the world.

I watched as the future arrived, bright and new, full of promise.

Newspapers, headlines in bold black type, spoke of the world's first nuclear submarine, the USS Nautilus, setting sail.

Ed Murrow's face looked at me, staring through the tiny black and white television screen, and told me another group of U.S. soldiers, acting as advisors, had arrived in a distant country with a strange-sounding name, Vietnam.

Disney Land opened, and a remarkable (and crazy-brave) young black woman named Rosa Parks refused to give up her seat on an Alabama bus

I remember the heat and sweat, the windless, listless days, but the summer stays with me for another, more terrible reason.

The reason has a name, and the name is Billy. He was my cousin, my friend. Billy joined the National Guard that summer and came to spend the summer months with us while he went through his basic combat training at Fort Chaffee.

Billy's arrival changed my life, marking the beginning of my lifelong, self-imposed, but inescapable isolation from other people.

I was seven the summer Billy showed me that the world was older, blacker, and far less hopeful than I imagined.

The summer of '55 never strays far from my thoughts. The long, hot days and terrible nights live forever in the hidden corridors of my mind.

Billy was a monster, a sexual predator; his perversions stole our innocence and ravaged our souls. Mine and my little brother, Gene's.

He tormented and abused us. We were innocent children betrayed by a trusted and favorite cousin. He was a heartless pedophile hiding in plain sight wearing the innocent face of friend, companion, family.

He exploited us in unspeakable ways in the sanctuary of our home.

Do you think it strange that I remember the deeds here, in the present, almost 70 years later, but cannot see his face? I think it is. Why can't I pull a clear image of the bastard into my mind?

Billy killed my little brother that summer. Just as surely as if he had forced the sleek, black barrel of a freshly oiled Colt 45 into his mouth, the weapon bursting Gene's lips and breaking his teeth, the front site settling into the back of his throat, choking off his cries as Billy, with an evil smile, pulled the trigger.

All that long, dismal summer, Gene and I hid whenever we could. Often, we'd climb to the roof of the old, once-bright-red, now pale-pink barn late in the day. We sat high above the earth, hidden from Billy and the world. We didn't talk about him and what he did to us, not one time.

Perhaps the talking was just too fucking hard or understanding each other's hearts; we didn't need to. We sat together, looking out at the world that betrayed us, one we didn't recognize anymore.

The rooftop became our favorite hiding place as other summers came and went. We sat up there, side-by-side, without words, breathing the fresh twilight air, being together with our memories, our broken hearts, and each other.

That sad summer changed my brother too. Sometimes I wonder why fate was kinder to me than him.

I still recall little Gene sitting up on the barn with me, wordless, gazing out at the distant hills called the Boston Mountains. I wonder if he was thinking about how we might escape the abuse even then. I guess I'll never know the answer.

If only I had been older, stronger, or wiser back then. Maybe I could've done something, anything, that might've helped my little brother.

It's not what you think. Gene didn't lose his balance and slip-slide off the old shingled roof as I tried, and failed, to reach out, snatch him by the arm, and pull him back to safety. He didn't stand on trembling legs, stumble to the edge, and topple off, although I believe he thought about it, as did I.

My little brother, his anger and despair overwhelming, often stood on the peak, hands held high above his head, shaking his fists and screaming wordless outrage at the world.

I would see him shrieking and rejoicing at his fury. After all, I had joined him in the screaming more than once. His final scream came down in the early fall of 1955.

He was never the same after that last primal scream. He was emotionally distant and increasingly erratic after that day. Thinking back on the changes I saw in him, I understand his hopelessness, and the faint sound of a distant gunshot echoes through my mind.

Gene didn't die for another forty-four years, but Billy took his life that summer just the same. Gene spent the rest of his life running from the memories, first into the U.S. Army, then as an itinerant preacher down in Mississippi.

After his preacher-man phase ended, he traveled the south for months wearing his U.S. Army dress uniform and singing for drinks in whatever bar or club would have him.

The Army tossed him out for bad behavior after less than six months. When he wasn't preaching at Grandma's church or on the streets of rural towns and small villages, he was usually in jail for being drunk and disorderly.

Billy never left his mind.

After enduring years of agony, Gene found peace in life's ending. His lifelong dance with risky behaviors caught up to him, and he died a slow, painful death. Cancer got him in the end, but to this day, I believe Billy's aim was true, his bullet of abuse fatal.

My cousin was the beast that has always lived in childhood nightmares. He was the boogeyman lying under the bed, the monster hiding in the closet, his glowing red eyes peering out, always watching, waiting for his chance to snatch you up and carry you to his filthy lair.

As I remember the long, lazy days of June and July 1955, I can still feel the heat. Each day sizzled, the sun a blazing ember high in the sky, not a cloud in sight. You get the picture if you can imagine living atop a BBQ grill.

When Gene and I managed to shake off the heat-induced lethargy or a stray breeze, like a breath of fresh air, granted us temporary relief from the withering temperature, we would play catch or spend an hour fruitlessly watering the dying garden in the afternoon sun.

Even with the slightly diminished heat, I could feel the sunbeams eat into my head and tunnel into my body, like hot rivets penetrating not steel beams but skin and muscle. The heat bored deep into the bones of my shoulders and back.

The only relief came as rare summer rains, the raindrops cooling our bare skin. For a few precious minutes, summer was delightful once again.

Even the slim elms and mighty oaks surrounding our home surrendered to the heat. Their withered, yellowed leaves hung limply from each branch. If they had the power of speech, they would've screamed for water or mercy.

Gene and I would have cried out for mercy also if we had only known how. I can't speak of the horrific sexual acts Billy demanded we do to him, that he did to us.

I locked those episodes away in a tightly sealed little box, much like a burglar-proof safe. Then, I forced the small safe into a lost corner of my mind, and there it stays, safely tucked away.

On an otherwise unremarkable day during that summer, Billy's rape (because that's what it was – rape), something changed inside me; some mysterious function inside my brain woke up. I can't tell you accurately when I became someone different. Someone other than I had been or the person I was born to be; I can't name a day or a time.

I only know that it happened.

While he was fucking my body and mind, his actions tripped a switch hidden deep in my brain. A strange new mechanism awakened, allowing me to walk out of my dreams and into another universe.

Amazing fantasies filled my nights, visions of life as another person in a different world. Were they a way to run away from the bad man and what he was doing to us? Good dreams erasing a terrible reality? I thought so back then and continued to think so for far too long.

Only shadows of the sexual acts remain with me, resting in the bottom of my lockbox like the rotting garbage from a grimy landfill.

Still, sometimes dim fragmented memories sneak up on me in the middle of the night.

I wake up, and in that secret timeless moment between sleep and full awareness, I feel the touch of his oily skin against mine and hear the echoes of his whispered demands.

On the worst nights, I struggle and moan as my memory recreates the feeling as his fingers pry open my mouth, and he slides his stiff, hard dick down my throat, all the time whispering to me that this is what cousins do if they love each other. It is normal, it is good.

Then the memories retreat, banished from my mind. My refusal to view them pushes them away, and they vanish, leaving only a blank space where they once lived. I MUST NOT remember. The memories might crack open my soul and leave nothing of me at all if I do.

Beyond those generalities, there is nothing. The despicable specifics of the ordeal are gone, safely hidden away.

Their existence, denied for so long, has retreated to the far corners of my mind and become dim shadows hidden away in my brain's secret folds and crevices.

Unwilling to look them in the face, I sometimes mutter to myself, "memories can't kill a person, can't destroy their mind or their concept of who they are."

Except they might. I think they will.

Those horrible memories (I feel them, even now, beating at the foundations of my will, demanding freedom), if set free, will extend the blight living in my soul until nothing's left but blackness, dark as a moonless night.

All I knew then, all I know now, is Billy left me with a hidden, diseased place in my heart. That piece must always remain concealed from the world. It can never be let out.

The little lockbox isn't perfect. Sometimes, even now, late in the night, the door springs loose. The box starts to leak a little around the edges, and those disgusting memories begin to spill out into my sleep. They leave me huddled under the covers and shuddering in the dark.

I become aware of someone, a person, or maybe, horribly, a *thing* is loose in the room. Some horrible entity is there, coming for me, reaching out for me even as I sleep. Paralyzed by fear, my heart hammers in my chest with a sound like the thundering hooves of wild mustangs in flight.

My mind, disciplined and made strong over the years, is unwilling to tolerate the memories. So, when they invade my nights and start to become too explicit, a mighty voice in my mind screams denial.

My consciousness crams the memories back inside with an irresistible force of will. As the little vault slams shut, a sound like far-off thunder echoes inside my head.

The combination dial spins wildly; thin wisps of smoke drift skyward as the dial speeds up, and glows an angry red from the friction before the door settles, firmly closed. I am safe for another night.

My brother could never find a box like that for himself. Little Gene, a small boy torn apart and reassembled into a small, ragged shadow of who he once was. Broken by abuse, he was always troubled, always *in* trouble. He suffered all the years of his life.

You might wonder why we didn't tell our parents. Sometimes I do too.

It is simple. Telling about Billy was not possible.

We had become small, shattered creatures, and, in our childhood innocence, some deceitful and undeniable part of us believed we were at fault. Ask any child who's been a victim of sexual abuse; they will say the same.

Talking about Billy was too hard for us. Speaking the words aloud was far too heavy a burden. The communication path between parent and child was too fragile a bridge to support the story Gene and I had to tell.

Hate, deceit, and shame entered my life for the first time that summer. It was the year betrayal raised its head and took away trust, built the wall (brick and mortar, four feet thick and high enough to touch the sky), separating me from the rest of the world.

I came into 1955 a typical boy, smiling, happy. But, by summer's end, I had transformed into an outsider, a child unable to trust, fearful and alone, hidden inside myself.

Betrayal: what an insignificant, miserly word. Far too small a word to encompass the damage done to a child, their body soiled, their soul forever blemished.

An altered reality hangs around their shoulders, like a shroud, for what's left of their life. No word describes the disgrace or the ache in their soul. Not in any language.

No one could live through what happened to Gene and me. Not without becoming someone different from who they were meant to be. Not when they are so young and innocent.

It cost Gene his life. His loss of innocence and his shame were too high a price to pay. I still miss him. I wish I could have found a way to provide him the comfort he needed to put it behind him and move on. I don't know how. I couldn't put the abuse and shame behind me; how could I expect to help him do what I couldn't?

The monster started chasing me through my nightmares that first summer. They continued for the rest of my life. But that summer and the following years right up to my pre-teens became so frequent and dreadful I started thinking about just stopping everything, ending a life I could no longer stand.

Looking back, I think I might have harmed myself had the dreams of a different and better life not finally arrived. The visions started when I was 12 and did not come as often as the nightmares, but often enough to give me some peace.

They continued off and on in the following years. They always appeared when family gatherings forced us to be close to Billy, near enough for the sexual corruption to continue.

At first, the images were small and short-lived but as accurate and authentic as life itself. Then, as the dream unreeled, I left my sleeping body behind and stepped into a new world.

The world I entered was not always the same. Sometimes I was a young boy running and playing on a neat, green lawn, the smell of newly cut grass heavy in the air.

A friendly golden retriever ran by my side. I knew the dog; the dog knew me. We were friends, brothers of the heart.

I heard his panting breath as he ran and rolled in the grass beside me, felt his long, silky fur tickling my nose and his long, wet tongue as it kissed my face. We were alone in this place; the dog my only playmate. Sometimes he chased me. Other times, I chased him.

On other nights, I walked into a world without the dog. Sometimes a young girl was there. She was small, dark-haired, sitting on a wooden swing, waiting for me. I walked to her, and she smiled. I stood behind her and pushed the swing ever higher; she flew skyward, and her laughter filled the air.

Many other times, I wandered into a vacant world. The only occupant of this universe, I sat alone in the long grass of an otherwise empty prairie, eating watermelon on a hot summer day.

Escapest dreams or desire for a different life? Whatever they were, I cherished them and held them close to my heart.

Billy's abuse and Gene's plunge into darkness left me a quiet man, slow to talk, even slower to show emotion. I became, in every aspect, more of an outsider as I grew older. Some thought me a cold, emotionless man. I don't believe I was. I was simply the hidden man standing outside the circle of life.

It was like God had picked up a piece of chalk and drawn a giant circle. Inside the sphere, close to the edge, he (or she, if that is your preference) placed family.

At the center, beyond my reach, he put the everyday people you meet at work, in storefronts, the people who knock on your front door selling home security systems, magazines, or Jesus.

Just outside the circle, he put me. Always on the outside looking in, like I didn't belong with the rest of the world.

I tried so hard and, sometimes, moved inside the circle in small, cautious steps. I never made it more than a few paces over the line. Each step cost me a great and uncomfortable price.

It took me too long to figure it all out. For the longest time, most of my life, I believed the visions were an escape from the real world.

Nevertheless, they were precious to me, and I looked forward to their infrequent appearance all my life. Alas, I grew old before I started to believe in the reality of my dream world.

It was a box of old childhood photos I had found that started me down the pathway to belief. They tickled my memories and led me down a trail of discovery. Momma had tucked them away inside my dad's discarded cigar boxes.

She sealed the cigar boxes with packing tape, then stacked them neatly into an old wooden apple crate, now cracked and splintered with age. I inherited the busted container and the photos after she passed away.

They helped me begin to understand my dreams. A small stack of notebooks tucked away inside my old Army footlocker helped too.

I had let the photos and notebooks lay in the bottom of the old trunk, gathering dust, for far too long.

I'd carried the footlocker with me all over the world, throughout my military career, from my last days in the steaming jungles and torrential rains of Vietnam to my final assignment in Germany.

Over the years, I packed the sturdy old box with notepads. My scribblings filled each spiral-bound book with enigmatic thoughts pulled from countless science books and magazines.

Inside those lined pages, I placed my thoughts on everything from the birth of the universe to the prospects of cold fusion.

My hobby was learning as much as possible about the various sciences. You might even say my time reading, researching, and compiling ideas was my hiding place. Part of me believes you would be correct.

Time inside the books (lost inside my thoughts) was like living in another world, separate and far away from the past I wished to forget – or ignore if forgetting turned out to be impossible.

Some of the concepts were difficult to understand at first, but the new ideas and theories I read about caught my attention and infected my mind. Studying them, I learned as much as any layman could.

The photos and the ideas captured in my notebooks gave me my first hints of what my dreams/nightmares/visions might mean. The idea came to me late one July afternoon as I sat in the attic riffling through the pieces of my life.

My attic, like most, was small, dirty, and miserably hot. So, I bushed away the dust bunnies littering the floor and the spider webs that hung from the rafters and clung to my face and clothes.

As I worked to clear a space, sweat ran down my back, leaked into the crack of my ass, and dripped off the end of my nose.

Wiping the sweat from my brow, I sorted through the cigar box photos and years of long-forgotten military memorabilia. It was the hottest part of the day. I shouldn't have been there, not by myself.

For a minute, I felt woozy and thought I might pass out. Later on, I did.

A handful of those old photos, black and white, faded and torn, yellowed with age, came from when I was a child. I couldn't have been more than five or six. In them all, I was laughing, running, and playing.

As I looked at those photos, echoes of the past rushed in. Sissy's voice calling out, "Olly Olly Oxen Free," tumbled through my mind. I smiled at the memory.

My smiles and laughter, captured forever in a single instant of time, were displayed in four-by-four squares of photo paper. Right then, the person in those pictures could've been the happiest boy on earth. But, the images that came later, when I was almost a teen, were different.

Most were pictures of my sisters twirling batons, wriggling their hips as they tried to master the hula hoop, or picnicking in the lawn. Only a handful featured me with a friend or classmate.

The smile was missing in those pictures. I wasn't grim, and I don't recall being unhappy, but the smile had vanished, replaced by a quiet, stoic vigilance.

There was always a distance between me and the others. The photos captured me watching as the others played. I was frequently sitting a few feet away, often at the edge of the yard, my back against our grand old magnolia, or sitting on the porch steps. I leaned against the garage wall or one of the heavy fenceposts in some pictures, watching from a distance.

I was never with the other children, never a participant. When I looked at the photos, I remembered the stance, recognized the vigilance sparkling in my deep, blue eyes.

The happy, laughing boy had disappeared, replaced by an adult in a child's body. I was a policeman, guardian, soldier standing sentinel over the others.

I wonder now if my mom – the picture taker in those days – had noticed, and if she had, what she might have thought. It's another answer I'll never find.

In other photos, from later in my life, when I was a grown man with children of my own, I was always apart from the rest of the family.

In those old pictures, I might be standing in the kitchen doorway watching as the kids helped set the Thanksgiving table or beside the fireplace mantle while Becca and the kids gathered around the Christmas tree.

Over the years, I tried to free myself from the shackles of isolation. Success in that effort, a rare occurrence, was cause for a brief private celebration – the colorful balloons and fireworks contained only in my imagination with just a tiny, fleeting smile displayed that others might see.

I believe my kids understood a little of my struggles, the way kids know so much more than we adults think they do. They knew how much I loved them; I am sure of that fact, though they often joked hugging me felt a little bit like wrapping their arms around a fence post.

One photo, my favorite, displayed a day of success. The picture, taken beside the clear blue waters of Cove Lake high atop Mount Magazine, showed me sitting in the sand a short distance away from the other kids, looking off into the distance as they jumped and splashed in the cool mountain water.

I still remember that day. It was one of my best. For a few minutes that seemed like hours, I joined the kids in the water, splashed it into their faces, laughed with them as they tried to climb my back and dunk me. It was a good day.

In most of the photos, I didn't appear at all. I was, instead, the photographer, the watcher. Always on the outside, looking in.

Late in the day, the attic heat sucked the energy from my mind and body. Ignoring the heat and weakness, I set aside those boxes of my momma's photos and the thoughts that went with them and dug into the bottom of the footlocker.

I reached for the locker, now a faded, dirty green, grasped the leather strap, and pulled it close. I snapped open the once shiny brass locking hasps (tarnished and worn, they had no shine left to them but were almost black with age) and lifted the lid.

Inside were the marbled, black and white notebooks I had filled with my writings over the years.

I sat in the attic dust and leafed through the books while my mind was on the hateful summer of my childhood.

As the attic grew hotter and the heat siphoned away at my energy, eating at my life, I thought about Billy, Gene, life and death, and my dreams.

I must have lost myself in the past for an unknown time as I sat alone in the heat, musing on the long ago. It seemed like minutes but could have been hours.

Hell, I was somewhere so far away there could've been time for the glaciers to melt, the sea to rise, and sweltering heat to take over the Earth as the sun emerged from its teenage years and became a red giant.

I might still be there if the neighbor's mutt hadn't started yipping at the mail lady. Shaking the lethargy from my mind, I thumbed through the notebooks. They were all present, dated, and labeled. The labels, all in block print, the deep black of a Sharpie, with titles like "Many Worlds Theory," "Quantum Vibrations in Microtubules," and "Quantum Effects in Biology."

The strange, almost supernatural notions in those last two sparked the idea I have. They started me thinking about that summer. Could trauma and loss have rewired my brain, creating a pathway to . . . where? Sanctuary? Peace? Home?

The idea grew in my mind and took root there. Might my nighttime visions not be dreams at all but something different, some strange connection to the quantum world?

An odd thought, but getting old and knowing the end of life is closer than the beginning, understanding death lurks around a not-so-distant corner can make anyone have irrational ideas. It can make them reach for a lifeline.

Leafing through those notebooks, I recalled that the dreams became more precise and more frequent as I aged. The boy in the yard disappeared, replaced by a man forever searching for something he could not name.

By my mid-twenties, one dream came more often than others. Pieces of it still flow through my mind even today. It goes like this:

Barefoot, I walk across a playground, like those found at any city park or elementary school in the U.S. The playground equipment, swings, teeter-totters, and monkey bars sit together, encircled by deep, soft sand, warm as a late July beach.

Walking to a swing set, I sit down and look toward the heavens to see a sky partially obscured by drifting clouds. Twilight's soft purple glow was fading as the total darkness of night slowly crept in. A few scattered stars flicker like fireflies through gaps in the clouds as they are torn apart and reassembled in strong winds far too high above me to feel.

There's a school building in the distance. Like many schools you might find in American suburbia, it's a blocky one-story affair, red brick, windows like watchful eyes reflecting the starlight.

Close by, a dark-haired girl walks my way. Like me, barefoot in the sand. She wears a long, full dress. It brushes and tumbles the grains of sand as she comes toward me, swaying and dancing across the playground.

Her dress, the color of cold starlight, shimmers as she walks, casting sparkles of dim moonlight. Each pale spark, reflected off the pale crystalline sand, flares into the fading twilight and then quickly disappears.

She comes to me, fingertips tracing my face. She bends her head to mine. Her hair, black as the empty void between distant galaxies, envelopes me as I look up into glittering sea-green eyes. Her ruby lips find mine, and I taste sweet surrender. I recognize this girl. It seems I have known her forever.

Legs astride me, she leans in for another kiss; tears flow from her eyes, and thin streams of black mascara follow the tears, running down her pale cheeks. She doesn't speak but suddenly leaps up, turns, and runs across the sand.

Jumping off the swing, I try to follow. Little sand-fingers reach up, pull at my feet, slowing me down. I struggle to break free, but the living sand holds tight to my feet, slowing me. I am too late.

The green-eyed beauty reaches the side of the building, turns, flees down a grey cement staircase, and disappears.

Following her, I gain speed across the sandy ground, finally reaching the stairs. I leap down, feet hammering a solo beat against the stone. I hit the bottom step to find – nothing.

She's gone, vanished like she never existed at all. I turn to my left to find a single door. The door is as black as her midnight hair with a gleaming silver handle. I push the handle and step into – wakefulness.

The dream has left me. I mourn its departure but know it will return, the same in all aspects as it has all my life.

I am a curious man, infatuated with science. All sciences but the weirdness of quantum mechanics (think entanglement and quantum tunneling) and the mystery of mathematics (the deeper you go, the more you begin to understand that the numbers connect, one to the other, in strange and unsuspected ways) have always been my favorites.

The known laws of physics border on the impossible and suggest magic is real and loose in the world. Or so I have always believed.

All my life, I've spent my spare minute and hours with my nose in books (as might be expected of a man isolated from humanity.) Along the way, I read everything I could find on astronomy, cosmology, astrophysics, the rise of life on earth, and the origin of the human species.

Once upon a time, when I was young, I thought I might become an astronomer, physicist, or mathematician, but then the Vietnam War came along, snatched me up, and set me on a different path.

Remoteness from others enveloped me during the summer of Billy and remained part of me all my life. Detachment defined me and became a career when I joined the Army just a handful of days after graduating high school.

I fit better in the military than anywhere else in life, never leaving once I joined. Perhaps it was the structure associated with Army life. The fact no one stayed in my life very long suited an outsider.

Moving to a new base every year or two and leaving old acquaintances behind to find new fit my outsider lifestyle. People in my life came and went with a frequency that accommodated a life lived outside the lines of that damned circle. You know, the one built by God (or a god), the one that contained everyone in the world but me.

My military specialty aided in my separation from others. I was a member of the Army's elite Signals Intelligence team, the Army Security Agency. The Agency encouraged its members to remain distant from anyone not part of the team.

We couldn't risk accidentally saying something classified. Our work was top-secret; silence our watchword. We watched and listened from remote outposts all over the world, capturing and analyzing streams of electronic signals from enemies and potential enemies.

We stole their secrets, plucking them from the electromagnetic spectrum, stripped them of complex encryption, and compiled intelligence reports.

After completing the task, we sent them to the highest echelons of the intelligence community.

We were the silent, secret warriors of the cold war guarding against the day some unseen enemy might strike. Our teams stood watch 24 hours a day, 365 days a year. Just as in my childhood, I was a lonely watcher, standing aside, looking for danger, and trying to protect those who couldn't defend themselves.

That sums up the story of my life; a soldier with a deep love for the mysteries of science. I became an intensely private man, and a stranger to most of the world, even to family more distant than wife and children. I was an outsider who did his best for those he loved and was loved by in return, but an altered man, damaged and made less by abuse.

I know what you're thinking right now. "Christ, that crap was a lifetime ago. You are an old man now. What happened to you was over 65 years ago.

Let that shit go; quit carrying it around like a fucking badge. If you can't let it go by yourself, see a therapist, get some fucking help!"

My answer is, "some things can't be let go. You're stuck with them whether you like it or not. Oh, and I did see a therapist. Twice a week for two years. It didn't help!

I still remember Billy, and I still hate that creepy asshole. If he's still alive (it's possible), God forbid, he'd be somewhere n his 80s now. If he's dead, great, the world's a better place. There it is. You don't have to like it, but that's where I am."

Glad that's out of the way. Now, where was I?

My old footlocker traveled the world with me. Over the years, as odd, fairy-tale ideas came to me, I scribbled them into my notebooks.

Quite a few of my odd ideas blossomed long after my childhood, and much of my adult life had come and gone.

After I retired from the Army, I put the notebooks and footlocker away. My singular focus was on learning to live, work, and play as a civilian by then.

Then, just a few years ago, my father died. My mom followed him into the unknown less than five years later, just as I celebrated my sixty-ninth year. Their deaths made me think about whatever it was the future might hold for me.

Kids grown and gone, left widowed and alone with my wife, Becca's, death the year before, just days after momma passed. There was no one and nothing to ease the fear. So, I reached for those old notebooks filled with years of my thoughts and half-formed ideas. They had long been my treasures, so I returned to them.

That may be why I didn't stumble upon this strange new idea 'till I was right here near the end of my life.

The day I spent alone in the sweltering heat of my attic, a thought came to me, a wholly formed and beautiful possibility. As crazy as it is, I believe it offers me a final escape from the memories of Billy. It gives me a place to go leaving behind the shame and the loss of a piece of myself. I have found a place where I no longer need to be an outsider.

And, yes, the notion that I might have lost my goddamned mind somewhere along the way did enter my mind. You will think so, too, and hell, perhaps I am.

I stayed too long up there in that dusty old attic, reading through my books and reliving my life, both the good and the bad of it. The suffocating heat sucked the life out of me, I guess. I must've fainted.

Laying on the grimy attic floor, I dreamed. The good dream that came to me then, the best one of all, the vision that has invaded my nights, visited me when I needed it the most so many times throughout the years.

I often tell people I never dream. The claim is crap, of course. Everybody does. I happen to be one of those folks who have little memory of the everyday dreams passing through my mind. Most blow away like ground fog in an early morning breeze.

They are all but forgotten as soon as I open my eyes in the morning. Most of them vanish like that, but some don't.

A couple of them play out like scenes from a movie. In them, I am an active participant. I experience color and sound, touch, and smell.

They aren't jumbled and jagged like scenes from a movie reel spinning out of control. Instead, events move logically from one point to another as they so often do in real life.

Some recur each year, often multiple times in a year. The sense of reality in this one dream is so strong it mimics ordinary day-to-day life.

It has been with me for as long as I can remember, the majority of my adult life. The idea that another chance at life exists comes from this dream.

It came to me once or twice a year when I was a young man, hardly more than a teenager, coming more often as I got older.

The vision has visited me as often as four or five times a year since I clocked in around my mid-forties. Sometimes it is insistent and comes to me more than once a week.

I expect you to think my idea a bit crazy, not something I should talk about, not where people can hear what I have to say. Maybe it is, maybe it isn't. I believe telling it now is essential. I think the time for telling someone is growing short.

I'm convinced the dream's connected to what comes after I'm gone. If anything's out there but the empty dark of death.

My spirit, unable to heal from the wounds of sexual abuse, clung to the refuge of my wonderful, mysterious dreams. Now I wonder if it is conceivable my dreams are not dreaming at all but something else, perhaps a visit to the world that might have been. I believe it might be so.

The dream I experienced lying there among the dust and debris of my too-hot attic was the one I have most often, the one that makes me think most of an alternate reality.

It always begins the same:

Midway through the night, my mind cloaked in the complete darkness of deep sleep when the dream comes to me and fills my mind.

When the familiar vision begins, I watch the last shreds of darkness slowly dwindle as the sun comes up over the nearby mountains. It is the very first moment of a newborn day. Blackness gives way to shades of gray and, then, to the faint pinks of early dawn.

As the sun breaks the horizon, I walk up a broad tree-lined driveway, through the open gate in a stubby picket fence (white, of course), and follow a narrow flagstone path to a house. The house is always precisely the same one. It is always on an early spring morning.

The house, made of redwood timber topped with cedar shingles, is magnificent. When I see the house, excitement overcomes me. My soul, filled with hints of awe and joy, cries out in relief; emotions overwhelm me.

A chill runs up my spine. The hair at the nape of my neck rises as if teased by an electric current or, perhaps, softly brushed by an unseen hand.

Something remarkable is happening. I'm here, but NOT. It is as if someone else, an unseen person, is walking, and I see the world through their eyes.

Dozens of rose bushes in as many colors smother the south side of the house as I somehow knew they would. The roses twine about each other as they climb their way up tall trellises; the morning air is sweet and heavy with their scent. Refreshed by the chilly air, I am glad to be alive, happy to be there.

I recognize the place, know it well, and feel I have treasured it for unremembered lifetimes. My dreams have brought me here before.

In the far corner of a vast yard, amid the grass just beginning its transition from winter brown to the pale greens of spring, stands a massive weeping willow.

The tree is easily ninety feet tall. The drooping limbs, overloaded with fragile new leaves, brush the ground in a circle at least forty feet across.

The flagstone path snakes its way around and through flower beds, small pines, and willows.

The trail leads me to a set of four wide steps, smooth redwood planks matching the house. At the top of the steps is a low, broad porch.

The porch, enclosed by a thick, waist-high rail, holds several wicker chairs and a porch swing. The swing, once white, is worn and weathered by years of use: the bare wood peeking through in several places.

The swing is sturdy and big enough for four adults.

Without understanding how the knowledge came to me, I know that when I walk across the porch and open the front door, I'll see a great room filled with soft couches and overstuffed chairs, some leather, some not, all in shades of faded tans and pale browns.

My mind conjures a bulky mahogany table that sits in the far corner of the room. In the near corner stands a spiral staircase made of some coffee-colored hardwood I don't recognize. Deeply polished, it twists and turns its way to the second floor.

I know nothing more about the interior of the house. My vision never extends beyond the large porch, the south-side lawn, and the big room's interior.

Often, when I glance inside, the room is filled with people. They smile and wave and say hello in the various ways old friends do when they meet again after a long absence.

If they exist, I never catch a glimpse of other parts of the house. My vision does not extend to other rooms, other people, or other things.

Each time, in every instance of the dream, emotion overwhelms me when I first spot the house. My mind is whipped about, twisted, and battered like a palm tree in a hurricane.

I am filled with an urge to beat the ground with my fists, cry like a baby and sob out the loneliness that has filled me up and eaten away at my spirit all my life. I tremble like a newborn fawn.

For a moment, I feel weak, like I might fall to my knees, my body exhausted by the sudden, overwhelming feelings. I don't understand what causes these emotions, but their power is staggering.

But I don't cry, fall, or do anything.

Instead, I stand still, statue quiet, weathering the emotional storm.

I do nothing because, at that very moment, I looked to the porch and noticed *her* standing at the railing, coffee cup in hand, watching me. I understand that she waits for me, as she has waited for uncounted hours and days.

Her hair is black as a moonless night, like the feathers of a raven's wing. Her eyes are green as polished jade, with lips like ripe strawberries. When I look at her, I recall past visions. They flow through my mind, dreams within dreams.

Now I am sure. I've come here before, each time in the early morning with the dew on the grass. And, each time, the dark-haired woman is there, waiting.

The soft winds of early spring always gently tossing her hair. She is forever standing on the porch, waiting for me. I know her name as soon as I see her and whisper it to myself, *Jenny*.

A memory emerges from the depths of my mind – I know the faintest flavor of wild honey will linger on my lips when they touch hers.

The instant I see her standing there, my heart beats faster, and my spirit aches with love, yearning, and wistful thoughts of belonging.

My eyes mist with tears, and deep in my soul, I realize this is my place, where emptiness is banished. I have finally come home.

As soon as she comes into view, my knees stop their trembling, and anguish vanishes from my heart. My need to tear at the earth and scream at the endless sky all come to a sudden, quiet end.

I walk up the stone path, my pace increasing with each step. I leap up the stairs. The beautiful woman who waits falls into my arms, her mouth urgently seeking mine. We kiss. A faint scent of wild honey fills my nose. The sweet flavor lingers on my tongue when we part.

She leans back from my embrace, palms against my shoulders, looks up into my eyes, and says, "it's been forever; where've you been for so long?" As she speaks, my lips mirror the words. She's said these words before; I've done this before.

I search for a response to her question and can't find it. Then, as if seeking an answer, I turn away from her and glance across the yard. I look towards the colossal willow, the rose bushes, and the entry gate.

I wonder what the answer might be, hoping to find it as I gazed at this beautiful place. Memory provides no solution. I see no explanation in my mind or this familiar place.

This world I have come to is small; it ends at the fence. Beyond that, nothing exists except a roiling black cloud of darkness.

The cloud shot through with white-hot arcs of flickering, blinding lightning, rolling toward me. I turn back to the woman called Jenny and start to speak, but there isn't time.

The dream fades, breaking up as the thick, black cloud roils the air, rolls over the fence, across the yard, and speeds toward me. Jenny, the house, and the grounds vanish into the storm.

As I topple into blackness, I reach out to her and scream at the pain of hundreds of lost and lonely days. My heart aches for the house and the girl who always waits.

I always wake from the dream with tears in my eyes, my hands clenched into fists as I try, and fail, to keep it with me, clear in my mind.

This dream has visited me many times over the years. Still, I don't understand what it means. I've never seen the redwood house or the girl, not in this life. I am not the man in the vision.

Could it be I'm conjuring a vision of the next world, or am I, momentarily, seeing life as it might have been had Billy never come into my life?

The dream is always like a small piece of heaven, not the heaven you read about in your bible. Angles don't run around braless, wearing sheer t-shirts and tight black jeans.

Paintings of angels show none with high, firm breasts and nipples like small stones when they press against your chest. No angels stood on the porch. There was no golden throne, and not one single voice sang hosannas. Nevertheless, I knew I had visited paradise.

I struggled with those thoughts, trying to understand the doubt and desire overwhelming my mind.

As I got old and understood death was waiting for me somewhere up ahead, had I let fear control my mind? Had I fooled myself? Was I reaching out for something more, something that surely must come next?

Was I giving my dreams more power than they had, seeking refuge from death?

I have not found relief in religion over the last few years. Although I do believe there is something out there.

I know some force formed this world and the universe that holds it. I'm pretty sure it's not God or at least not all-seeing, all-knowing being thought of by most people.

Momma took us to church every Sunday morning and Wednesday night. Still, the Supreme Deity and I are strangers to each other. We parted ways back in '68 in a place called Phubai Combat Base.

Never in my life have I recognized any sign that the divine person I heard about in Sunday school is running the universe or that he cares much about what we are doing down here.

But I can tell you this: I don't believe death is the end. I think something follows death. A man can dream and, in dreaming, find hope. Can't he?

The beautiful, dark-haired girl doesn't exist in my life. She only appears in the dreamscape of my mind. I have a theory about the dream, though. It sounds a bit foolish, even to me, but I like the sound of it anyway.

The man isn't me. I don't think he is, anyway, not the person living here in this world. I believe he and I are related, if related is the right word. He is part of me, or I am part of him.

While I cannot prove anything and probably never will, my heart realizes the truth.

I imagine the dream world I've found is bound together more closely with me and my everyday life than the average person can understand.

I'm a practical person, or so I always believed. I suppose that can't be true, not anymore. I believe those recurring dreams show me a life I might have had. I become part of the dreamworld in some strange fashion. This place I see and visit in my dreams could be the world where I belong. How is that possible?

Could it be Billy's sexual exploitation of us left me with a tattered, tarnished soul that created an imaginary world where I am safe, sane, and not alone?

I think that's what happened. Somehow, my childhood trauma, or the need to flee from it, created a pathway between my world and another. It is a world I can only visit when I dream.

The path between here and there is not constant but periodically becomes accessible only when my conscious mind shuts down, and I drift into a deep sleep.

This other me was luckier than I was. The man in the dream, my mirror image, lives in an alternate world where Billy didn't penetrate the mouths and asses of a child with his moldy, smelly penis. Maybe in this other universe, Billy never existed at all.

I think my dreams are attempts to go to this safer, better place, to a life where Gene is still alive, where we shared a childhood unmarred by Cousin Billy. The thought passes through my mind regularly these days.

Although I believe in the idea, a small part of me thinks it is a fantasy, an escape to another world that never was and never will be. Perhaps I'm wrong about everything? Sometimes I think I am.

If I'm right, the ugliest event in my life, the sorrow and agony of Billy, his rape of my mind and body, combined with the grief of my brother's death, changed me. The change gave me a great gift. I was gifted the ability to leave this world behind for a brief time.

Know this: the price I paid for this gift was too high.

I think again of my life. Tragedy and joy, loss and gain, sorrow and delight, all sewn up a tight little ball of twine together. One unimaginably depraved man changed everything in my world over the course of an otherwise forgotten summer.

We all realize we're marching toward death from the moment we're born. That knowledge is neatly tucked away in some forgotten space in our minds and is rarely thought about or examined. The closer to the end of my life, the more I'm looking for an anchor to hold, something that frees me. I need some reason or rhyme for the things that happen and a way to escape those things forever.

We all know the past is unchangeable. Still, I want to believe it is and that I have found a way.

I should have told my mom and dad about Billy. I know that now. I should have been a stronger, better man who could have been closer to my brother, Gene, held him tight, and loved him harder.

I should have tried harder to have friends, to fight off the belief that I did not belong, and to embrace the world instead of avoiding it. The circle holding me back was too substantial, too strong. I could never find a way to step that far across the line God drew. Damn her soul.

When my time comes in a year or ten or longer, I fear I will find that I was wrong about everything. Belief is hard to sustain, and I desperately want to believe, but I wonder if I have constructed something from nothing. The grief and pain, eating away at me for all these years, building an imaginary refuge in my mind?

Have I fooled myself into believing a better life waits somewhere? We all know the answer to that. I got old, and long after the time to let go of the past and erase Billy from my mind had passed, I created a fantasy of what might have been.

That makes sense. Do I really believe it? No! I hang on to my fantasy.

I wonder:

Will I wake from death to find myself standing in front of Saint Peter, the Virgin Mother, or Allah, the Gods I have denied for so long?

If so, I fear they will be holding a "No Vacancy" sign high above their heads—the words written in large, blood-red letters.

Will I not wake at all but be consigned to the darkness of eternal oblivion, remembered briefly and sadly by my children before fading away into nothingness?

Or will I wake on an early spring dawn, tasting crisp morning air heavy with the scent of newborn roses?

Will I open the gate and walk along a familiar path cobbled with stone, taking me to the one who waits?
Will I ...

END

About the Author

I read a lot of books. Most of the "About the Author" segments I've read are written in the third person.

I started to copy that theme here, but it feels more than a little weird to me. So, let's do it this way.

Here I am, a 74-year-old man, twice retired; once from the U.S. Army and once from a career as a computer network engineer.

Now I sit alone in the dark writing stories for you.

I joined the U.S. Army immediately after completing high school. The reasons were simple, we were at war in Vietnam, and I thought it was the right thing to do. Odd as it may seem, I still do. Besides, my choice was to join or get drafted.

I spent over 20 years as a member of the Army's elite Signals Intelligence unit, the Army Security Agency. Stationed in different locations around the globe, we listened to the communications of our enemies and stole their secrets.

After retirement from the Army, I spent another twenty years designing, building, and maintaining global computer networks.

I have self-published three books. One is a semi-autobiographical novel of my experiences as part of a Top-Secret military experiment in psychic warfare. Self-published on Amazon under the title *Secret Warriors, Psychic Spies: Redux*.

The second is the one you just finished, a group of unusual short stories.

The third is a follow-up to this one. *Strange Stories II – The Empty Earth*. It is only two stories, but both of them are long enough to be callednovellas.

The focus is on climate change and what might happen if it accelerated rapidly. It is also my vision of what *will* happen if we, humanity at large, continue to do nothing.

When not writing, my wife, Judy, and I spend our time playing with grandkids, camping, or traveling across the U.S. visiting our beautiful cities and national parks.

I have found it takes as much courage to write a book or story and then to submit the work for someone to review (essentially giving it a grade) as anything I have ever done. Writing is hard work.

Most of my stories are fiction mixed with a bit of truth and spiced with bits and pieces of imagery from the world of dreams and imagination.

If you read (and like) any of these books, please leave a review – it's important. If you purchased the paperback version, lone it to a friend when you're done or, better yet, drop it off in one of those little neighborhood library boxes that seem to pop up everywhere these days.

RWM –
Morrison, CO
February 2022

CPSIA information can be obtained
at www.ICGtesting.com
Printed in the USA
BVHW051108110723
667064BV00012B/1058